THE LOVE KILLER

the L

JOSH MCDOWELL & BOB HOST

TYNDALE HOUSE PUBLISHERS, WHEATON

Visit Tyndale's exciting Web site at www.tyndale.com

Designed by Dean H. Renninger

Library of Congress Cataloging-in-Publication Data

McDowell, Josh.
   The love killer : answering the question "Why true love waits" / Josh McDowell and
Bob Hostetler.
      p. cm. — (The powerlink chronicles)
Previous edition published as The love killer : a novelplus. Dallas : Word Pub., © 1993.
Novelization of message contained in adult-level book, Why true love waits: a definitive work
on how to help your youth resist sexual pressure, by the same authors.
Summary: Relates the experiences of Krystal Wayne and her friends at Eisenhower High as they
struggle to understand the relationship between love and sex. Includes follow-up material on the
biblical concept of love and how it applies to our daily lives.
Includes bibliographical references.
   ISBN 0-8423-6590-7
   [1. Christian life—Fiction. 2. Conduct of life—Fiction. 3. High schools—Fiction.
4. Schools—Fiction.] 1. Hostetler, Bob.   II. Title.

Printed in the United States of America

06 05 04 03 02
5   4   3   2   1

CONTENTS

Acknowledgments · vii

01 Krystal with a K· 1
02 James Bond and Eisenhower High · · · · · · · · · · 21
03 The Couple in the Clearing · · · · · · · · · · · · · 39
04 The Education of Brad Stuart · · · · · · · · · · · · 57
05 Falling In and Out of Love · · · · · · · · · · · · · 73
06 Stalled by the Side of the Road · · · · · · · · · · · 85
07 Washed Up and Washed Out · · · · · · · · · · · · 105
08 Date for Debate · · · · · · · · · · · · · · · · · · · 119
09 Arming for Battle · · · · · · · · · · · · · · · · · · 143
10 The Great Debate · · · · · · · · · · · · · · · · · · 165
11 The State of the Debate · · · · · · · · · · · · · · · 187
12 Winners and Losers · · · · · · · · · · · · · · · · · 213
13 An Ice Party · 229

Notes · 235

ACKNOWLEDGEMENTS

We want to acknowledge the excellent team that collaborated with us to bring this work into being. We thank:

- Marcus Maranto for providing valuable research on sexually transmitted diseases;
- Suzanna Rojas-Thompson and Andrew Steger for their valuable insights on critiquing the original manuscript;
- David N. Weiss for his creative input in molding and shaping the novel's storyline;
- Steve Griesinger and Teresa Cummings for their input and evaluation on debate techniques;
- Nigel Horridge for enlightening us on British culture that helped make the character of Brad Stuart realistic;
- Jamie Puckett for her expert rewriting of various sections for this new revision;
- Dave Bellis for conceptualizing the storyline, writing numerous sections, and creative design of the NovelPlus format.

Josh McDowell
Bob Hostetler

KRYSTAL WITH A K

Something Jason Withers said made Krystal laugh so hard she had to hold her hand over her mouth to contain the drink of soda she'd just taken.

Jason slurped a mouthful from his soda can, puffed his cheeks in imitation of Krystal, and pressed his nose almost against hers, his eyes wide in feigned panic.

Suddenly Krystal jumped up from her seat around the campfire and rushed to the trees. She returned a few moments later, red-faced, wiping her mouth and coughing.

"Thanks a lot, Jason," she complained. "It went up my nose and everything."

"What did I do?" he asked in an attitude of perfect innocence.

Krystal slapped his shoulder feebly and picked up her soda can from the ground beside her. She began to take a sip of soda, but, eyeing Jason suspiciously, set the can back on the ground instead.

"What's so funny?" asked Amber Lockwood, who sat on the other side of Krystal.

Krystal shook her head. "Nothing," she answered, rolling her eyes at Jason.

Krystal, Jason, and Amber sat around a blazing campfire at Gilligan's Lake with more than a dozen others from Westcastle Community Church's growing youth group. It was two weekends before school started, and Liz and Duane Cunningham, the leaders of the youth group, were hosting an overnight outing just like last year's. The day had been filled with swimming, boating, and water skiing; now they all sat around the campfire and took turns telling funny stories.

Amber sat next to her boyfriend, Will McConnell, who had started the stories by relating how he had lost his swim trunks while waterskiing last year. Next to Will were Darcelle Davis, Buster Todd, and Joy Akiyama, three seniors who had been among the leaders of the youth group in its transformation last year into the "Liberation Commandos," a group of Christian students committed to finding new ways of sharing their faith with friends at school.

The circle around the flickering fire included some faces that hadn't been part of the group at last year's outing: Hillary Putnam, who had come to the group through her friendship with Amber; Kim Holmes and Debi White, two members of the rally team; and Greg Hooper and Billy Maxwell, who had graduated last June and now sat next to Reggie Spencer, who had helped them trust Christ.

"How many here remember the time that Jimmy Hodges got sick in his birthday cake?" Joy Akiyama asked. "He started feeling kinda queasy toward the end of his party at that restaurant, so he just took what was left of that supermarket cake his mom bought for him and—"

Several in the circle had started giggling as Joy talked. Krystal, however, had stopped smiling at the mention of Jimmy's name. She remembered. In fact, Krystal reflected, the others around the circle had no idea how well she remembered. Only she knew the truth about Jimmy Hodges. No one else had been as close to him as she had.

*   *   *   *   *

Krystal had met Jimmy Hodges at a Halloween party in her eighth-grade year. She had worn a long, skintight black dress with full sleeves and a slit up the side. She'd dyed her hair black and parted it in the middle to look like Morticia Addams. Her mother almost didn't let her leave the house; Krystal knew she thought the costume was too "mature." But Krystal didn't feel mature after she arrived at the party, just a little silly: *I'm not tall enough to be Morticia*, she thought.

"Nice costume," Jimmy said. He'd just walked up to her from halfway across the high school gym. He wasn't in costume. His short brown hair was perfectly combed, and thick eyebrows shaded eyes that looked unblinkingly at her. The eyes combined with captivatingly full and colorful lips, almost too beautiful for a guy's face, to form an irresistible combination. "You from Westcastle?"

She nodded a response, followed with a soft "Uh-huh."

"I don't remember noticing you before." His eyes caressed her admiringly. "And I always notice girls like you."

"I'm, uh—" She didn't want to say it. She broke his gaze and looked aside. "I'm in eighth grade." She could feel herself blush. She stole a quick glance at his eyes, still fastened on her, then looked away again.

Behind him a handful of people were dancing. But most of the students were clinging to the walls or hovering around the refreshments.

"Eighth grade?"

Krystal's heart sank. She glanced at him and saw a flash of hesitation. It was gone in an instant, though, and he eyed her from head to toe and up again.

"I would never have guessed you were in eighth grade. You look *really* mature for your age."

She smiled and followed his gaze. He wasn't looking at her eyes.

"I'm Jim," he continued. "Jim Hodges. I'm a junior."

A *junior!* Krystal opened her mouth. A *junior! He's practically in college*, she thought. Finally she let a weak "Oh" escape her mouth. *He's a junior and he said I look really mature for my age. And it doesn't bother him that I'm only in eighth grade!*

Krystal had flirted with boys; she'd even had "boyfriends" before. Last year, her mom said she could go to a movie with Justin Mitchell as long as *she* went with them. Krystal had begged her mom to drop them off and let them go alone. No go. Mom did, however, agree to sit at least six rows away in the theater. But Justin had clung to Mrs. Wayne like glue, and when they settled into their seats for the film, Krystal's mom somehow sat between them. Krystal forced Justin to promise never to talk about their "date" at school.

She gazed at the party going on behind Jimmy Hodges. It seemed that everywhere she looked she saw pretty girls standing alone, older and taller girls, girls who looked like high school sophomores and juniors. But Jimmy wasn't talking to those other girls, not even to the blonde that Krystal recognized as a rally girl. She drank it all in and let it warm her like a sip of hot chocolate on a snowy day.

He was still looking at her, in the eyes now, and she waited for him to say something. But he acted like he was waiting for something.

My name! Oh yeah, I haven't told him my name.

"Krystal," she blurted, and knew at once that it was too sudden and too loud. *Softer, stupid. Get a grip*, she told herself. "Krystal Wayne."

"Krystal." He smiled.

"With a K," she added, wondering immediately if she should have said it.

"Krystal with a K," he echoed. "So, Krystal-with-a-K, do you want to go for a walk?"

She half-shrugged, half-nodded her answer, and Jimmy slid his hand lightly around her shoulders, then placed it in the middle of her back as they walked together to the exit.

They walked slowly around the parking lot. The music and other sounds of the party still carried clearly beyond the walls of the school. Jimmy talked and asked Krystal questions, which she answered shyly. He draped his arm over her shoulders, then gripped her tightly around the waist, then rubbed circles in the small of her back with the flat of his hand.

They came to a stop between a tiny pickup and a dark two-seater sports car. Jimmy turned Krystal to face him with her back against the car. He leaned in close and shot an intense look into her eyes before closing them to kiss her.

The kiss lasted only a moment. They parted. She shivered and crossed her arms in front of her.

"It's chilly," she said. Her voice quavered. "I forgot my coat."

He kissed her again, lightly, quickly.

"Why don't we go for a drive?" he whispered.

She nodded, afraid that if she tried to speak again, he might notice in her voice the strong emotions his kiss had stirred in her.

He reached around her and opened the door.

"No," she said. "Wait."

He held the door open.

"My parents are supposed to pick me up," she explained, thinking as she said it how childish it sounded.

He looked at his watch. "What time?"

"Uh, well, eleven o'clock."

"Great," he said, as if there were no problem. "We'll come back before then. We've got plenty of time."

Krystal hesitated, but his smile convinced her. She slid into the low seat of the car and gathered her long skirt in her hands while Jimmy closed the door.

He sped recklessly to Brackett's Ledge, overlooking Rising Sun Park. The car slid to a stop and Jimmy cut the engine.

The lights of Westcastle glittered below, and the stars above, as if the sky were the surface of a silent lake, reflecting the white and yellow lights of the city. They sat for a few moments in silence, until Jimmy stretched his arm around Krystal's shoulders and she leaned into his embrace.

They talked softly and kissed often, each kiss becoming longer and more passionate and their sentences becoming shorter and less frequent.

Finally, Krystal broke off a long kiss with a start.

"What time is it?" she asked, knowing even as she asked it that the news would not be good. They'd been sitting there a long time.

Jimmy looked at his watch in the dark, then shifted in his seat and reached for the control panel. He switched the light on and examined his watch again.

"Uh-oh. It's after midnight," he said, reaching for the key.

Krystal's mom, dad, and sister Kathy faced her as she closed the door behind her.

"Where have you been, young lady?" her mother greeted her. "Do you know what time it is?"

Her dad stomped over to the large picture window and pulled the curtain aside, but Jimmy's car had already pulled away. "Who was that?" he demanded.

Oh great, Krystal moaned inside herself. *Tag team.*

"Kathy was there at eleven o'clock to pick you up," her mom continued, "but there was no sign of you. Where were you? Who were you with? What were you doing?"

"We just—"

"We?" Her dad jumped in. "Who's 'we'?"

"Will you let me talk? I mean, I'm hardly even in the door and you all gang up on me." Krystal hadn't moved from her position in front of the door.

"Who were you with, Krystal?" Her mother took a turn. Krystal imagined Mom and Dad in a big-time wrestling ring, one slapping the other's hand for a fresh shot at their opponent.

"I went with Jimmy—"

"Jimmy?" her mom asked.

"Jimmy Hodges."

"Jimmy Hodges? Who's this Jimmy Hodges? Where do you know him from?"

"Just some boy. I met him at the party, okay? All we did was—"

"You mean you didn't know him before tonight? Where's he from? Where's he live?"

"Was that him driving the car?" Her dad pointed toward the window. "How old is he?"

Krystal strode between her parents and sister and stopped in the center of the living room. She whirled to face them.

"I don't know where he lives." Krystal was surprised at her own answer. "I *just met* him."

Krystal twisted her shoulders and shook Kathy's hand off. "Nothing happened, okay? I met Jimmy, we walked around the parking lot for a while, and then we went for a ride." She had their attention now. No one interrupted her. "We just *talked*, okay?" She paused a moment. "We didn't realize how late it was. He brought me straight home when we saw that it was after midnight. That's all."

"That's all?" Her mother's voice pierced Krystal like fingernails on a chalkboard. "Krystal Marie, when we take you somewhere like a Halloween party, we don't expect you to go driving off with a boy. We trusted you to stay at the party."

"Look, I'm sorry, okay?" She was nearly screaming now. "You act like I did something really terrible. All I did was go for a ride and you—"

"You watch your tone of voice with me, young lady!" Her mother matched her volume. "You can't talk to your mother like that!"

"You're right, Mom! I *can't*. That's the whole problem. I can't talk to my mother, I can't talk to my father, I can't talk to anyone, because all you want to do is yell at me and I'm sick of being yelled at!" Krystal wheeled around and ran up the stairs to her room. She flung the door closed behind her, sat on the edge of her bed, and yanked a tissue from the fuzzy box on her bedside table.

When Krystal heard her bedroom door click open, she knew it was her sister. She dabbed her tearful eyes and blew her nose without looking up. She felt the bed sink as Kathy sat beside her.

Kathy waited a few moments before speaking. "They'll cool down, Krystal. They just worry about you."

Krystal eyed her sister. "Why do you always take their side? Why can't you just *once* be on my side?"

Jimmy called her the next day, Sunday, and Krystal told him the story of the night before.

"They told me this morning," she said, forcing the words out. "I'm grounded for a month." Her stomach tightened as she said it. She feared that this would ruin everything. She had the idea that if they couldn't see each other for a whole month, it would all fall apart and she would lose him.

"That's rough," he said. They talked a while longer, but Krystal hung up feeling that Jimmy would find someone else, some girl who wasn't grounded. Someone prettier—and older, probably.

Krystal drooped all the next day at school, thinking constantly of Jimmy. *I should have known*, she told herself. *There's just no way he could really like me. He probably thinks I'm a little kid, especially from the way my parents treat me. Why would he want to go out with me when there are all those girls at the high school who are older—and more "experienced"—than me?*

She thought she recognized his car parked by the flagpole when school let out that afternoon, but the driver's seat was empty. Then she noticed him, walking toward her. His thin frame made him seem taller than he was.

He greeted her with a kiss and a strong arm around her waist. "How long's your lunch period?"

The kiss and the question surprised her. "Uh, 11:30 to 12:15," she answered.

"Good. I'll pick you up tomorrow. Right here."

He met her every day that week and the next. Krystal would slide discreetly out the side door of the cafeteria, through the doors at the end of the hall, and into Jimmy's waiting car. Sometimes they would sit in a parking lot or walk together in a park; other times they would find a secluded spot where no one would disturb them.

On Friday of the second week of her grounding, her parents came into her room. Krystal knew immediately by the serious looks on their faces that they had found out what had been going on with her and Jimmy. They had also discovered that he was almost seventeen and a junior in high school. After another shouting match, Krystal's father counted off his decrees on his fingers.

"One, you will not see this Jimmy Hodges again. Two, your grounding is extended for another month. Three, you will be eating your lunch in the guidance counselor's office until we have some reason to start trusting you again."

Krystal cried and shouted protests, but her parents stood their ground stubbornly. "I can't believe you're doing this to me. You're acting like I committed some horrible crime." She stormed over to the telephone.

"What are you doing?" her father asked.

"I have to call Jimmy to tell him, don't I?"

"No," her father answered. He snatched the receiver out of her hands. "You're to have no contact with him at all. If he calls, I'll tell him that myself. I'll tell him a few other things, too; I can promise you that."

The next few weeks became a gray, frozen landscape for Krystal. She hadn't seen or talked to Jimmy since their last lunch period together. She didn't even know if Jimmy had called or if her father had talked to him.

Her grounding was almost over when she made her decision.

She stuffed a few articles of clothing and other necessities into her bookbag one morning and tossed a cheerful "good-bye" to her parents as she left for the school bus.

She never reported to class that day. Instead, she trudged the distance from the middle school to Eisenhower High. The weight of her overstuffed bookbag seemed to increase with each step, but she eventually plunked it down on the sidewalk in front of "Ike."

Leaving her bag where she'd dropped it, she trotted through the parking lot, seeking Jimmy's little black car. When she found it, she ran to it and tried the handle; the door opened. She returned to retrieve her bag and flung it onto the driver's seat before sliding in and closing the door.

She sat and dozed and dreamed the day away in Jimmy's car. She watched for him when the lunch periods began and students streamed from the exits and rode off in their cars while others hung around outside or walked beyond school property to pass a cigarette around a tight clump of people. When the crowd had completely trickled back into the school, however, Krystal still sat, chilly, alone, waiting for school to let out.

When the door on the driver's side finally creaked open, Krystal sat up, surprised. She uttered a sound somewhere between a grunt and a word. Jimmy pushed her bookbag off his seat and against her thigh.

"I guess I've been asleep," she explained, moving the bag to the floor at her feet.

"What are you doing here?" he asked. He held his door open and sat only half on the seat.

She searched his eyes and tried to read what he was thinking. "I ran away," she answered.

He looked unblinkingly at her and seemed to hold his breath. "To where?"

"To you," she said.

They both fell silent again, and she felt a twinge of fear of what he might say. She lowered her head slightly, then managed to break his gaze. She stared at his right shoe, which rested against the brake pedal.

"Wait here. I'll be right back." Jimmy sprung from the seat of his car so fast she thought he might have hit his head. She watched him stride over to the edge of the parking lot. He approached a girl with short brown hair, shorter than Jimmy's, in a denim jacket. He turned her with a hand on her arm so they were both facing away from the car. They seemed to talk for a few minutes, their heads close together, and Jimmy turned around and jogged back to the car. The girl disappeared around the corner of the building.

Jimmy spoke again when he had pulled into traffic. "What do you want to do?" He paused. "What happens now?"

"I don't know, I just had to get out of there and I had to see you. I thought maybe you'd have an idea."

Jimmy swerved to avoid a car turning left and jerked the car back with two swift moves. Krystal's gaze never strayed from his face, but he seemed engrossed in the traffic and didn't meet her eyes.

"Jimmy, didn't you miss me?" she said finally. "Did you try to call me or see me? Didn't you wonder how I was doing or anything like that?"

He glanced at her shortly. "Yeah, I did. Of course I did, Krystal. I'm just surprised to see you, that's all." He looked back at the road. "You ran away, huh?"

"I've got a few things in my bookbag," she said. She began feeling uncomfortable. This was not how she had pictured their reunion. Her thoughts drifted to the girl in the denim jacket. *Maybe I messed up his plans for this afternoon,* she thought.

"You, um," he started, falteringly, "you have any friends you could stay with?"

Her head sagged slightly as she said, "No. My parents know all their parents."

"Relatives?"

She answered flatly, "Same thing. They'd never let me stay

without telling my parents." She lifted her head to look out the window and see where they were. They were on some side street she didn't really recognize.

"Well," Jimmy pronounced with an air of finality, "I guess we'll have to figure something out then." He pulled to the curb and jumped from the car. Krystal peered out her window at a ranch-style duplex with two garages in the middle. Jimmy opened her door.

"Bring your bag inside," he told her.

They entered through the back door, which was unlocked. Krystal looked around shyly at the kitchen, clean but cluttered. She started to lower her bag to the floor, but Jimmy strode to a door across the room and said, "Bring it with you."

He disappeared through the door and she followed, down the stairs to a paneled basement.

Posters—most of them picturing heavy metal rock groups— covered the walls, and an unmade bed extended from the farthest wall. Clothes, food wrappers, CD and cassette covers and a large bottle of aftershave littered the floor. Wires draped around the walls and over the floors, leading from distant speakers to a massive stereo system in one corner.

"I can straighten this up a little," Jimmy said, shoving a pile of objects against the wall.

Krystal tiptoed to the bed, sat, and balanced her bag on her knees. Jimmy stood before her, as if each of them were waiting for the other to move or speak.

"You can stay here," he said. Then he added, slowly, "For now, anyway."

"What about your parents?"

"It's just my mom. She'll be home late tonight. She hardly ever comes down here." He looked at her wide eyes staring at him. "I may even tell her. She's not like most parents."

"What will she do?"

"Depends on what I tell her. But she doesn't interfere too much with things I want to do." He sat beside Krystal, slid an arm around her shoulders, and pulled her against him. "She'll be okay with this."

Krystal sat motionless in his arms. *This isn't how I pictured things*, she thought, and immediately accused herself, *How did you picture things?* She realized that she had no answer for that. All she knew was that hiding out in Jimmy's basement didn't feel quite as liberating as she had hoped.

But when Jimmy kissed her, all the warmth and excitement she had felt a month ago flooded her emotions. She sat, practically motionless, as Jimmy set aside her bookbag and helped her slide off her coat. He leaned in to kiss her again.

"Wait a minute," she protested gently, realizing she didn't like where this was headed.

"What's wrong?" he asked between kisses.

She didn't want to break the closeness they were feeling, but she wasn't comfortable with what was happening. "I just . . . I just don't know if I'm ready for all this."

Jimmy gently brushed her hair away from her face. "Krystal, I'm just trying to show you how much I love you."

Those words felt so good. Krystal couldn't remember the last time someone had told her she was loved. Still, she hesitated.

"What's the matter, Krystal?" Jimmy asked, beginning to sound frustrated with her. "I thought you loved me, too."

"I do," she whispered.

"So then what's the problem?"

What was *the problem?* Krystal wondered. Her mind was a maze of contradictions. She hadn't planned on things going this far, but Jimmy had been so good to her and she didn't want to let him down. She knew this was something her parents wouldn't approve of, but she and Jimmy really loved each other and sex was just an expression of her love. So how could it be wrong?

"Come on, Krystal," Jimmy said, a little more forcefully. "If you love me, why don't you show it?" He reached over and opened the drawer beside his bed. "You don't have to worry; I *always* use protection."

Krystal had so little time to think, but her will to resist diminished at each turn. Finally, with no apparent reason to refuse, she smiled weakly and nodded. She let it happen then, not unwillingly, but with a mind racing with fear and apprehension.

She stayed with Jimmy for five days that seemed to her like an unreal dream. It was romantic at times, almost like playing house when she was not much younger. He would leave in the morning to go to school while she stayed behind and watched television or listened to his CD collection. They ate in Jimmy's room, either food he brought down from the kitchen or a pizza he had delivered. They went for a ride in the car every evening, but stayed away from places where she might be seen.

She saw Jimmy's mother only once in those five days, the evening of the second day, after Jimmy told her about Krystal. She came downstairs and greeted Krystal unenthusiastically, sleepily.

"She kinda has her own life," Jimmy had explained.

With each day, however, Krystal became more depressed. She felt close to Jimmy, and when he kissed her she felt wonderful inside. But it felt more and more like his kisses were just his way of leading to the "real thing." Since that first time when he led her to his room and onto his bed, he didn't seem interested in talking or joking or doing fun things together; he only wanted one thing. She wasn't just getting bored; she was feeling used.

Krystal left a note on Jimmy's bed before she left. She knew she would face a scene at home and didn't want to endure one with Jimmy.

She didn't see Jimmy Hodges for weeks after that. He didn't call. She assumed he was mad, but when they finally did meet again, he smiled and chatted cheerfully.

⚫ ⚫ ⚫ ⚫ ⚫

The others around the campfire had changed the subject and were now talking excitedly about plans for the upcoming "See You at the Pole" event, when Christian students at Eisenhower High would gather before school for a circle of prayer and witness around the flagpole. But Krystal heard nothing of their conversation; she sat silently, remembering Jimmy.

Sometime after her brief romance with him, he and his mother moved from Westcastle and word came back to Krystal—she struggled now to remember how she found out, but that memory wouldn't come—that Jimmy had died in the middle of his senior year of AIDS.

It took her three weeks after she learned of Jimmy's death, but she went—alone, fearful, panic-driven, and humiliated— to a clinic and underwent a blood test herself.

The results came back negative, and she remembered Jimmy's words, "You don't have to worry; I *always* use protection."

Even now, surrounded by her many friends, Krystal shuddered. After Jimmy, things got worse and worse for her until she had not only had many sexual encounters, she had gotten involved with a rough crowd at Eisenhower High and had become one of the most successful drug pushers at "Ike," selling drugs she obtained (and sometimes stole) from her own father, who had begun using drugs himself.

All that changed last year, however, when she had become a Christian as a result of some of the people in the campfire circle. She sighed with relief.

It's bad enough just remembering all that, she told herself. *I could never have survived these last three years wondering, Do I have AIDS?*

JAMES BOND AND EISENHOWER HIGH

I can't believe I let you talk me into this." Krystal leaned over the aisle between the desks.

"What?" Jason Withers sounded indignant. "It's no big deal, Krystal. It's a silly debate team. We'll be great at it."

Krystal scrunched her nose up at Jason as if he had thrust a pair of smelly socks in her face. "It's just dumb for me to be joining the debate team, Jason. I'm a senior."

"Oh, so this is beneath you, huh?"

Krystal made an annoyed smacking sound with her tongue and started to speak, but Jason didn't give her the chance.

"Look," he said, "if you don't like it, you can leave me alone here." He jerked his head and rolled his eyes to indicate the rest of the students in the room. "With this group."

Krystal laughed. Jason sat in the desk next to her, wearing a T-shirt emblazoned with the words "Lord's Gym" and a drawing of the robed figure of Jesus wearing a crown of thorns and bearing a massive cross on His back. Another phrase beneath the illustration proclaimed, "Bench press this." Over the shirt he wore a camouflage army jacket and jeans ripped so widely at the knees that they appeared ready at any moment to break off and settle in a rumpled heap at his shoetops. His high-top gym shoes were bright red with green laces.

Eisenhower High was a large school, but Jason Withers had always found a way to stand out. He had a more active sense of humor than anyone Krystal knew and a flair for the dramatic that last year, in his sophomore year, had made him the star of the drama club.

It seemed to Krystal that, with a few exceptions, the other boys in the room all wore shirts with animals or letters on them. The girls wore plaid. She laughed again.

"Okay, Jason. I'll stick around. If only to protect you," she lowered her voice, "from *them*." She wiggled her eyebrows wickedly.

Mr. Detweiler cleared his throat loudly and began counting out groups of photocopied papers. He handed a sheaf to several people. "Pass them back as best you can," he said.

The voices in the room quieted as the students read the papers introducing them to the debate team and how it operated. Only the sound of pages being flipped over the corner staple punctuated the students' reading. After a few minutes, the silence was broken by a male voice in the back of the room.

"Are we ever permitted to choose the topic for debate ourselves," he asked, "or must it be assigned?" The question sang with the music of a distinctly British accent, proper and precise. Every head in the class turned.

He held his head slightly cocked and thrust into the air, as if his question still dangled from the end of his chin. His brown hair was perfectly combed, and his blue eyes shone with self-assurance as he scanned the faces of the people staring at him, some of them with wide, open mouths. His arms were crossed over a starched white shirt punctuated down the center by a thin black tie. His legs stretched long and thin from under his desk and crossed at the ankles.

Jason turned to look at Krystal. He watched her for a few moments as she twisted her neck to stare at the boy in the back without turning around in her seat. He thought he noticed a hint of an approving smile across her lips.

Mr. Detweiler arched his eyebrows. "You're not from Westcastle, are you, Mister . . ."

"Stuart," the boy replied. "Brad Stuart."

Jason and Krystal exchanged looks. Jason whispered to her again. "Bond," he said, in his best accent. "James Bond." Krystal cackled loudly and covered her mouth with a hand.

She looked at Mr. Detweiler. He had flashed her a glance but now was looking back at the new boy.

The teacher had begun to return to the front of the class, but he stopped between Krystal and Jason's desks and turned again. "I assume you have some suggestions, Mr. Stuart?" he asked.

"Oh," the boy answered. "Well. I don't mean to presume, sir, but may I suggest, em, whether condoms should be made more available in American schools. Just as an example."

Krystal and Jason shot each other a glance. A low hum of reaction drifted over the room.

Mr. Detweiler cleared his throat. "That would certainly provoke, uh, some stimulating debate." He cleared his throat again. "Yes." He seemed to grope for something to say.

"That's it exactly. I only mean to suggest stimulating topics. Such as the outdated Puritan ethic of sex and relationships between the sexes. Or even parental intrusion into adolescents' sex lives."

"Yes, thank you, Mr. Stuart." Mr. Detweiler wheeled again and returned to the front of the room. "There are really two answers to your question," Detweiler continued, slowly stepping down the aisle in the boy's direction. "It all depends on whether you're involved in debate or in I.E. In debate, the participating schools vote on the topics each year, so topics are not a matter of individual choice; in I.E., or Individual Events, you may choose your material. In fact, some individual events require original material. I suppose, however, that even in debate you're free to tackle any topic you choose." A sly smile snuck across his face. "If it's not the one you're assigned, however, you're certain to lose."

"Okay," the boy said, his courtly accent transforming the phrase into two distinct words. "Thank you."

A few students exchanged glances. One of the boys wearing a white shirt with a blue "D" emitted a soft, "ooh," at Brad Stuart's polished courtesy.

Mr. Detweiler cleared his throat once more and asked loudly, "Now, are there any questions about the material on the handouts?"

Krystal and Jason left the room together when Detweiler dismissed everyone and stopped in front of Krystal's locker.

Jason imitated Brad's accent. "Or I might propose a discussion of why sex is the only subject I can think or talk about."

"Shhh." Krystal looked up from fiddling with her locker combination and peered down the long hallway. "Not so loud. He might hear you."

"Or perhaps," Jason continued, "we could jolly well debate what makes me jolly well think so jolly well of myself, don't you know?"

"Stop," she said, slapping Jason's shoulder feebly. She pulled the handle on the locker and swung the door open.

"Well, I'm sorry," Jason said, "but he's just a bit much for me to handle. I mean, give me a break! Who does he think he is?"

She slammed the door shut and spun the lock. "You said it yourself, Jason. He's James Bond."

Brad was already the topic of discussion when Krystal met

Amber Lockwood and Darcelle Davis after school. Even though Darcelle and Krystal were both seniors in high school and about the same age, Darcelle seemed more like a big sister to Krystal. She was the first African-American girl to be elected president of the senior class at Eisenhower High. She was vice president of her class last year and a member of the National Honor Society. When Krystal first became a Christian in her junior year, Darcelle seemed to be around every time Krystal needed a shoulder to cry on. When things got so bad at home that Krystal had to get out, she moved in with Darcelle and her mom.

Amber was younger than the other two, but the three of them had developed a closeness in recent months as a result of their youth group at church and their efforts to lead their friends at school to Christ. Janice Hurley was the latest friend from school to develop a real, living relationship with Christ as a result of their youth group. Janice had been attending the big stone church on the corner of Vine and Simpson with her parents all her life, but just last spring Darcelle had led her in a prayer for salvation. She still attended church with her parents, but had become a part of what the Westcastle kids called "The Liberation Commandos," a group of students who met to pray for the salvation of their families and friends at school.

"Is he in any of your classes, Krystal?" Darcelle smiled like a toothpaste commercial.

"No," she answered. "I don't think so. I mean, I only noticed him at our debate team meeting."

Amber, the captain of the rally team, leaned her shoulder against Krystal. "Oh, so you *noticed* him, huh?"

"Stop. I didn't even know he was there until he asked Mr. Detweiler a question." Students still streamed around the trio as they stood outside the school entrance, cradling their books in their arms.

"Yeah, he does have a dreamy voice, doesn't he?" Amber and Darcelle exchanged meaningful glances.

"Will you two cut it out? Besides, Amber, you're not supposed to notice things like that. Will wouldn't be very happy." Will and Amber's relationship had been growing and deepening since last spring. They were one of those couples that everyone assumed would be together for life.

"I'm not saying *I'm* interested, Krystal. I just think maybe *you* are."

"I don't know where you're getting this stuff. I barely even saw the guy!" She remembered Jason making fun of Brad. "It's Jason, isn't it? He said something, didn't he?"

"Oh, so there *is* something to it?" Amber winked at Darcelle, who hadn't stopped smiling.

"No! Now, stop it. I'm not kidding."

Amber and Darcelle burst into laughter. Krystal's face reddened.

"You two are impossible."

"Okay, Krystal," Darcelle offered. "We're just kidding. Jason told us about your debate class. He cracks me up!"

"You have to admit, though," Amber said, "he *is* cute."

"Who, Brad?" Krystal asked.

Amber rolled her eyes. "Who do you think?"

"Well, I don't know."

"Oh, come on, Krystal. He's cute. What's the big deal about admitting he's cute?"

"Nothing, I just didn't think about it."

"You mean you didn't notice." It was a statement, not a question.

"Okay. All right, he's kinda cute, okay?"

Amber was enjoying herself. Darcelle seemed content to listen to her friends, her head bouncing from side to side as if she were watching a tennis game.

"You're telling me that if he asked you out, you'd say no."

Krystal let out an exasperated sigh. "I haven't even met the guy!"

"If he asked you out right now, you'd say no?"

"Yes! What's your problem, Amber? Why is this such a big deal with you?"

At that moment, Brad Stuart, who had just come through the school doors, stepped around Krystal. He nodded to Amber and Darcelle, then addressed Krystal. "Hello. It's Krystal, isn't it?"

"Huh?" All three girls were shocked at his sudden appearance. Amber's mouth snapped shut, and Darcelle smiled bigger than ever. Krystal just stared in astonishment.

"How would you feel," Brad began in his carefully clipped accent, "er, about sharing some burgers together sometime this weekend?" He paused, but Krystal said nothing. "Maybe this Friday?"

Krystal stood frozen in space and time. She might have

been a statue except for an occasional blink from her disbelieving eyes.

"I could call for you about, em, half past six, if that's all right?"

Amber and Darcelle craned their necks in Krystal's direction like robins probing the grass for worms.

Krystal finally broke the awkward silence. "Uh," she said. She opened, then closed her mouth, then opened it again. "Uh, yeah, uh, that'd be okay, I guess. I live on Whitewater Drive."

"Yes, I know that already. Good. Half past six it is. Friday. I'll see you then."

Brad strode off to the parking lot. Krystal stood between her friends as the three of them watched Brad walk away without looking back. When he disappeared among the cars, Amber and Darcelle turned simultaneously to face Krystal.

Amber spoke first. She cleared her throat and said, "You were saying, Krystal?"

* * * * *

A hairy form lumbered through the smoldering caverns far below Westcastle and Eisenhower High. This creature, like all demons of hell, possessed an ugly mutant body—a cruel, mirthless joke perpetrated by Satan on his followers, the angels who had rebelled with him and so lost their heavenly position.

The demon, whose name was Nefarius, inhabited a gorilla's body, matted with hair and smelling like a zoo. His demon eyes looked out from the head of a walrus, with one of his yellowed tusks broken jaggedly in half.

He limped through the ooze-dripping tunnels, humming a raspy, unidentifiable melody. The passage darkened as he progressed farther from the last intersection of tunnels until it was so dark he couldn't see a thing in front of him. He hit a wall with a dull thud and his nose and forehead dripped with the slime and soot that blanketed the sides of the cavern. He uttered a gargling curse, extended his hand to the scummy surface, and guided himself along the passage until he reached his destination.

Nefarius veered from the main shaft and hobbled through a rugged archway. He crossed the huge workroom on the other side of the archway to one of numerous openings in the wall and entered the command center of Subsector 477, which was thundering with activity.

A grotesque maintenance runt passed Nefarius, spearing him in the shins with the claws on the end of his scaly toes. Nefarius lashed out with his thick arms, but the runt was already far beyond him. He cursed again, then turned and surveyed the cave.

The cave had changed dramatically since the "Westcastle catastrophe," as the denizens of hell labeled the events of last spring. Ratsbane had been unsuccessful in breaking the "Powerlink" between the Holy One and Will McConnell, Amber Lockwood, Jason Withers, and others at Eisenhower High. As a result, the very chamber of Satan himself had been shaken and people like Krystal Wayne had been liberated from the domination of hell.

Over fifty glowing computer screens crowded the command center. A hideous mutant hunched at each screen, pounding the keyboard and alternately listening and growling responses over the microphone and headset that was clipped to each head. Bundles of cable snaked along the floor in every direction, leading to "the PIT," or Prime-Evil Impulse Transducer, a giant console of fifty-five small screens and hundreds of dials, buttons, meters, and lighted displays elevated on a platform in the center of the room. A barrier of metal railings circled the platform, parting only for the stairs that led to the cave floor below.

Gone, however, were the old, crude stone conduits that once stretched from the PIT's keyboard to the cave's craggy ceiling. The conduits once transmitted invisible impulses from the demons operating the PIT to the targets of Subsector 477: the students of Eisenhower High School in Westcastle. The stone pipes had been destroyed last spring by the prayers of the students and the intervention of heavenly forces in response to their prayers. A major renovation had installed a sophisticated broadcast system for transmitting evil thoughts and suggestions that allowed Subsector 477 of the Temptation Division a greater capacity to influence groups and families as well as individuals. The system had been developed and first tested in Subsector 90210 of the Temptation Division, which focused its diabolical efforts on specialized areas of Southern California.

The new technology transmitted demonic suggestions through radio waves that could often be picked up by dust particles or mold spores; the human ear received such airborne impulses and passed them on as thoughts, ideas, or vague impressions.

Nefarius ascended the stairs and approached the foreman.

"Report, you worthless walrus." Glowing demon eyes glared at Nefarius from the magnified head of a carpenter ant, which bobbed atop the warted body of a giant toad.

"Foreman Ratsbane," Nefarius said, groveling before the foreman of Subsector 477. "I have an urgent directive from Sector 87, your malevolence." His stubby fingers extended a small computer disk to his superior.

Ratsbane grunted his approval. He turned his head slightly to one side and spat on the floor of the platform, barely missing the other demon. Nefarius stared at the foul steam that rose from the red wad of spittle.

"I love these things," Ratsbane said, smiling at the diskette. He jerked his eyes up quickly to look at Nefarius, who stared back with a questioning look. "I mean, that is, I think they save me a lot of time and work." He locked eyes with Nefarius. "I don't love. I don't love anything. It's a figure of speech, and if you ever repeat it to any demon in hell, I'll make a snack of your eyeballs, you shaggy pile of worm waste." He drew his arm back as if to strike his subordinate, but Nefarius dodged and swung himself over the railing and out of Ratsbane's reach.

"Now," he creaked, as he watched Nefarius flee. He turned to the enormous PIT console and slipped the disk into a slot. "Let's see what this is all about," he said.

The computer clicked and whirred, the screen flickered, and a message flashed onto the screen in blood-red letters:

```
DIRECTIVE 27656

The mighty and dishonorable Therion hereby

directs that demon Ratsbane, formerly foreman of

Subsector 477, is reassigned to Subsector 1122,

there to train under the direction and supervi-

sion of Foreman Mallus. This transfer is effec-

tive immediately.
```

Ratsbane whirled from the giant console of screens on the PIT platform and reared his shiny ant head.

"Stygios!" he tried to scream, but his throat produced only a low croak, like a bullfrog's belch. He coughed angrily to clear his throat and tried again. "Stygios!" He generated more volume this time, but his voice cracked from a croak into a squeak after the first syllable of his assistant's name.

He pounded the PIT console. "Curse this degenerate mongrel body!" He squinted his glassy black eyes over the mutant bodies of the demons slaving away at the PIT terminals all over the cave.

Finally, the crooked pelican head and squat beaver body of Stygios, Ratsbane's assistant, appeared on the platform. His baggy beak swelled and shrunk with his heavy panting from running all the way from the cave entrance to the PIT platform.

"I am here," Stygios announced grandly.

"I can see that, you flat-tailed mass of steaming pig entrails," Ratsbane said. Stygios bowed his head slightly, a grin showing across his beak, and never took his eyes off Ratsbane.

"I've been reassigned," he informed his assistant. "I must leave immediately. You'll be in charge until my replacement is announced."

"Oh no, my former superior," Stygios answered. "Your replacement is here." He grinned broadly. "I am the new foreman of Subsector 477. You must leave my station . . . now."

▶ THE INSIDE STORY ◀
We Interrupt This Program

"We interrupt this program for a special news bulletin . . ."

Perhaps you've heard that announcement while watching television or listening to the radio. It means, of course, that the management of the station decided that certain information was urgent or important enough to warrant breaking into the regular program with a bulletin.

The book you're reading now is more than a novel; it's called a NovelPlus, a concept created specifically for the Powerlink Chronicles. The NovelPlus format allows the authors to break into the story at key points and present some important information in a section called "The Inside Story." You may be so interested to learn what happens next in the story of Krystal Wayne and her friends at Eisenhower High that you will be tempted to scan or skip these sections. Doing that, however, will deprive you of the full benefit of this NovelPlus, which is not only a gripping story, but also applies the story to *your* life.

If you read the first book in The Powerlink Chronicles, *Under Siege*, you already know some of the characters that were introduced in the first two chapters of this book. For those who have not met them (or need to renew their acquaintance), let's take a quick look at the group from Westcastle Community Church and Eisenhower High that calls itself the Liberation Commandos:

▶ **KRYSTAL WAYNE,** *senior:* rebelled against the image of a "perfect" older sister to establish her own identity, was into everything (drugs, sex, etc.) until she trusted Jesus Christ immediately after last year's campout with the youth group. A continuing struggle with low self-esteem presents the greatest challenge to her success as a Christian.

▶ **JASON WITHERS,** *junior:* always the clown, Jason kept his struggles and failures as a Christian secret until he and Will McConnell pledged to be accountable to each other. Since that time, his spiritual growth has taken off like a NASA shuttle launch.

▶ **DARCELLE DAVIS,** *senior, the smiling student leader:* lives with her mother, never knew her father. She had an abortion and a miscarriage during the eighth grade; became a glowing Christian at a summer conference before her freshman year.

▶ **WILL MCCONNELL,** *junior, the computer whiz:* lives alone with his mother. Has been dating Amber Lockwood for several months, which has helped him deal with strong feelings of rejection as a result of his parents' divorce.

▶ **AMBER LOCKWOOD,** *junior:* a rally girl who rebelled against strict parents, Amber committed herself fully to Christ after last year's campout and has shared her faith with many of her friends, including Hillary Putnam and Kim Holmes.

▶ **BUSTER TODD,** *senior, "army brat" and mechanical genius:* Buster grew up in a strong Christian family, moved to Westcastle as a sophomore. Though he doesn't have a flashy personality, Buster is calm and confident about sharing his faith.

▶ **JOY AKIYAMA,** *senior:* raised by adoptive parents who beat her and molested her; has begun dealing with her pain and anger, but dealing with her parents has not been as easy. She has forgiven them, but still spends as much time with her friends—and away from home—as possible.

▶ **REGGIE SPENCER:** Reggie graduated last year and was instrumental in his football teammates Tony Ortiz and Ty Coleman trusting Christ. Tony and Ty are now in college; Reggie works with Duane Cunningham in construction.

▶ **DUANE CUNNINGHAM,** *age twenty-seven, carpenter and volunteer youth leader:* Duane took over the leadership of the Westcastle youth group a year ago and guided, instructed, and discipled them as they transformed it into the Liberation Commandos, a group of high school kids committed to effectively sharing their faith with their friends.

▶ **LIZ CUNNINGHAM,** *age twenty-six, part-time sales clerk, full-time wife:* met Duane in a prayer group at college; Liz had a huge effect discipling Amber, Joy, Darcelle, and Krystal. She spends a lot of time now with Hillary Putnam, Debi White, and Kim Holmes.

These are not the only people you'll meet in these pages. Janice Hurley and Marlon Trask, for example, are Eisenhower High students who trusted Christ as a result of the Liberation Commandos' tactics. They participate in the youth group, but attend other churches.

And, of course, the denizens of hell—Ratsbane and his demonic associates—will also make appearances as they try to disrupt the

Powerlink between Krystal and her friends and God. As hell's diabolical plot unfolds throughout this story, you will see why the demons' prime directive is to disrupt the communication link (the Powerlink) between the Holy One and his children and keep it disrupted.

THE COUPLE IN THE CLEARING

Krystal winced as the screen door slammed shut behind her. She stood inside the kitchen, expecting her mother to call out.

Krystal had left home to move in with Darcelle Davis late last fall in order to escape a tense family situation—especially the influence of her drug-addict father. Since then she would occasionally drop in at home, usually trying to time her visits so she would miss her dad. And though she never stayed long, she always left with her stomach churning up all the old feelings and resentments.

She tiptoed through the kitchen and into the dining room. Her older sister, Kathy, sat at the middle of the table, her long, red hair gathered in the back with a richly colored scarf. Various colored papers and art supplies littered the table in front of her.

"Working on an art assignment?" Krystal asked. Kathy was a senior graphic arts student at Ramsdale College in town.

Kathy looked up from her work with a tolerant smile. "Hi, Krystal. I've been meaning to call you."

Krystal picked up one of the objects on the table and turned it over in her hand, examining it carelessly. She set it back down and slid into a chair. "What about?" She finally looked her sister in the eye.

"My wedding."

Krystal almost asked Kathy to repeat what she had said, then realized she had heard it correctly. The two sat looking at each other wordlessly for a few moments.

"Your wedding?" Krystal asked.

Kathy nodded her head. "After graduation. In June."

Krystal stared. There seemed to be two of her in the room: One Krystal was sitting motionless, unable to speak a syllable, and the other was frantically saying to herself, *Why are you just sitting there? Say something. Do something. Ask her a question.* She tried desperately to remember who her sister had been dating. *Have I met this guy?* she asked herself.

Since Krystal left home last fall, she had not contacted her parents very often, and she had talked to her sister even less. She'd always thought that Kathy was prettier, smarter—better in every way than Krystal could ever be. "She's always had it easy," she used to complain to others. "She's never had the kinds of problems I've had." Since becoming a Christian, Krystal had begun to recognize that part of the reason her sister had always seemed to have it easier was because she'd always been better than Krystal at steering away from bad decisions. Kathy never got into alcohol or drugs, always dated "nice boys," and hung around with what their mom always called "the right crowd"—which Mom always compared with Krystal's friends, which she called "the wrong crowd."

Krystal finally gave up trying to recall who Kathy's boyfriend was. "Have I met him?" she asked.

"Why, of course you have, Krystal," Kathy said. Krystal was amazed at how much her sister could sound like Mom. "Bill. Bill Fuller." Krystal still wore a blank look. "We've been dating for almost two years."

"Oh!" Krystal's memory suddenly kicked into gear like one of those monster trucks with twelve-story wheels. "Okay, I remember him. Yeah, Bill." *No wonder I forgot him,* Krystal thought. As far as Krystal was concerned, Bill Fuller wasn't just boring—he was practically comatose! He had come to Thanksgiving dinner when he and Kathy had just begun dating and Krystal had thought the whole family was going to fall asleep right at the table. The only interesting thing he did all day was when he picked up his plate and silverware to help clear the table and walked away, inadvertently dragging the tablecloth—and everything on it—halfway to the kitchen.

Kathy smiled that smile of hers again, a condescending smile that reminded Krystal of her mother. "Bill proposed to me a couple weeks ago, in class."

What did he do, Krystal thought, *pass you a note?*

"You know what he did? He passed me a note!" Kathy almost squealed. "He drew a beautiful little card and wrote a poem and passed it to me during the lecture."

Krystal closed her mouth just in time to keep from laughing. She screwed her face up into a serious expression and said, "That's beautiful, Kathy."

"Oh I know! Isn't it?" Kathy gushed. *Mom again*, Krystal thought. *I wish she could hear herself.*

"Anyway, Krystal . . ." Kathy's enthusiasm faded and her voice quieted. "I wanted to ask you . . ." Their eyes met again. They'd been looking past and around each other during most of the conversation. ". . . if you would be in my wedding."

The hairbrush in Krystal's hand moved so slowly that a cobweb might easily have formed on it. She sat in front of the mirror, readying herself for her date with Brad Stuart but thinking about her conversation with her sister Kathy. She pondered why she and Kathy were so different. Kathy was so much like their mother, and Krystal—*unfortunately*, she thought—was her father's daughter in so many ways. Most of their lives, the two had clashed: Kathy seemed always to be preaching at Krystal or trying to prevent her from doing something, just like Mom was always ranting at Dad. *I always felt*, Krystal reflected as she switched to another brush, *like I had two mothers—Mom and Kathy.*

She realized now, as she set the brush down and spun her head to look at the back, that when Kathy first popped the news about her upcoming wedding, Krystal hadn't even considered being a part of it. *I guess I would have attended, all right,* she told herself. *But why does she want me to be a bridesmaid? We haven't exactly been close. I mean, I did some pretty mean things to her before I became a Christian. I guess it's just something you do. If you have a sister, she's supposed to be in your wedding. And if your sister asks you to be in her wedding, you're supposed to say yes.*

Krystal was jolted from her thoughts by the sound of the doorbell and "Mom Davis," as she called Darcelle's mother, calling up the stairs. She studied herself in the mirror again. She had put a lot of thought into how she looked for this date with Brad. She wanted to look her best, but she wanted to be careful not to dress too well, telling herself, *This is just a casual date. I don't want to give him the impression that I'm taking this evening too seriously.* She wore a pair of black jeans and a white turtleneck under a red sweater. Two thin necklaces spilled over the turtleneck, one with a single pearl and the other with a silver dove in flight.

Brad held the door for her as she slid into his black foreign sports car.

"I've been looking forward to this evening," he purred before he closed her door. "It's my purpose," he continued in his syrupy accent, "to give you the most enjoyable evening possible." A moment later, Brad Stuart and Krystal Wayne sped off on their first date.

●　●　●　●　●　●

Ratsbane drew a sharp breath as he entered Subsector 1122. He had expected to see something like Subsector 477, so he was not prepared for the sight that greeted him. The physical arrangement of the PIT cavern was similar to the subsector he had just left, but that was the only similarity.

Everything is so shiny here, Ratsbane thought, remembering the dusty, dank cave he'd just left. Gleaming silver surfaces seemed to cover everything in the cave: desks, computers, machinery.

The Prime-Evil Impulse Transducer towered above its platform, three times larger than the one he had used in the old subsector. Ratsbane estimated that two hundred monitors dotted the face of the PIT console, and a huge keyboard like that of a pipe organ stretched across its bottom like a wicked smile. This new PIT model had no dials or buttons, but was scattered with toggle switches, finger pads, and colored lines of light.

Suddenly Ratsbane's attention was arrested by a dark figure that seemed to descend on him from the ceiling of the cavern. He let out a startled exclamation as the head of an enormous snake dropped before his face.

"Who are you?" the snake demanded. He spoke in a clear

voice with a faint hissing sound that was always present but seemed to come from the background, somewhere behind the words that were spoken.

"I'm—I'm Demon Ratsbane. From Subsector 477. I'm supposed to report to Foreman Mallus."

The snake drew back, and Ratsbane could see that the scaly head was connected to the body and neck of a huge heron, a water bird with long legs and broad wings.

"I am Mallus," the creature said. The snake-bird perched on a mechanized platform that swung out on a long, jointed arm from the base of the PIT console, allowing Mallus easy access to any of the screens, keyboards, or controls scattered over its face.

Ratsbane stood indecisively for a moment, watching Mallus swing to the PIT platform. Finally, deciding he was expected to follow, he hopped along in pursuit of the snake-bird.

Mallus glared at one of the screens on the panel of PIT monitors. "Who's responsible for this?"

"For what, mighty Mallus?"

Ratsbane turned to locate the source of the question and saw a huge headset with ear pads and a thin microphone fastened to a bony-plated armadillo head. Belchabub, the demon who had responded to Mallus's question, inhabited the head and body of an armadillo; the long tail, however, had been bitten off and eaten by an overdemon whom Belchabub had displeased. Now, without the tail, Belchabub's waddling walk would cause him to tip too far to one side and he would roll onto his back. A few pitches and rocks would eventually right him, but it was a source of endless frustration to him.

"I want to know who's responsible for this!" Mallus cried, aiming his finger at one of the screens.

"Is something wrong?" Belchabub sputtered.

"She's wearing a turtleneck!" Mallus pointed to Krystal Wayne's image on the computer screen and scowled at Belchabub, whose eyes stared blankly back.

Ratsbane, recognizing Krystal, felt a silly urge to shout, "Hey, I know her!" But he stifled the impulse as Mallus shouted again.

"She's wearing a turtleneck!" he repeated. "And a sweater over that!"

Belchabub remained unresponsive, until Mallus struck with bared fangs at his underdevil's head. Belchabub dodged the blow and stepped back just enough so that he would be out of reach if Mallus struck again.

"It's your job to catch things like that, you incompetent," Mallus hissed. "A turtleneck with a sweater over it! We might as well dress her in a suit of armor over a plaster body cast! How's our little British bulldog supposed to get her to do the deed when she's dressed like that? Get out of my sight!" He advanced on Belchabub again, but the underdevil dashed for the steps, lost his balance, and rolled down the staircase on his bony back.

Mallus peered at Ratsbane with reptile eyes. "You understand now why I need a new assistant. That's why you have been assigned to me."

Brad chatted easily all the way to the Four Winds Restaurant, asking Krystal about her family, her friends, and Eisenhower High. When she got out of the car and took his arm to walk into the restaurant, she realized the conversation had been all about her.

I don't think I've ever talked so much about myself on a date, she thought, *and we've only been together for fifteen or twenty minutes. He already knows a lot about Mom and Dad and Kathy and about me and all kinds of stuff. He must think all I do is talk about myself.*

As soon as they entered the lobby of the restaurant, Krystal felt self-conscious.

"I don't think I'm dressed for this place," she whispered to Brad, glancing at her jeans and black LA Gear shoes. The Four Winds wasn't the fanciest place in town, but it wasn't a hot dog stand, either.

"Nonsense," Brad whispered back. "You look lovely." Krystal noted that Brad wore slacks and a pale blue shirt with a striped tie—he didn't look out of place at all.

The hostess waved a couple menus in their direction and led them to a corner table, announcing as they sat down, "Your waitress will be with you shortly."

Krystal grasped her menu in both hands and laid it flat on the table in front of her. She leaned her head and shoulders across the table toward Brad and said, "Why didn't you tell me we were coming here? I'd have dressed a little differently." She realized that just a hint of irritation surfaced in her voice. *Well, I am irritated*, she admitted.

Krystal noticed, as she raised her head after giving thanks silently for her meal, that Brad was watching her closely.

"Is anything wrong?" she asked.

"No," he answered quickly. "No, not at all."

She lifted her fork and began eating her salad.

"You know," he began, "you Americans are, em, more forward about your religion than we Brits."

Krystal crunched her salad and curled her eyebrows to reflect her interest.

"Oh, yes," he continued. His salad remained untouched in front of him. "Americans talk much more freely about religion than Brits." He cleared his throat and nudged his salad plate to the side with the back of his hand. "I've noticed you're not frightened to tell others about your feelings. The British don't talk about their religion much; those who do are disdained as 'Holy Joes.'"

The waitress returned to Brad and Krystal's table and asked if everything was all right. They nodded and she departed. Krystal picked with her fork among the last few bites of her salad and set her fork down.

"What else is different over here?"

He considered a moment. "Well, when I started telling my chums that we were coming over, folks told me stories about what to expect from America, and I got it in my head that I wouldn't dare go out shopping on my own or even go out walking alone for fear of being mugged! Of course, I found out that's only true in a small percentage of America."

She smiled. The waitress returned and asked Krystal if she was finished with her salad. Krystal nodded as the waitress removed her plate; then she posed the same question to Brad.

"Finished?" he asked, wonder showing in his face. "I haven't even begun." He looked back and forth from Krystal to the waitress. "We've been waiting for our meals."

The waitress stammered a confused apology and scampered off toward the kitchen.

"What was that all about?" he asked Krystal.

"She was waiting for you to finish your salad."

"Finish my salad?" He looked incredulously toward the swinging kitchen doors through which the waitress had just passed. Suddenly, his eyes rolled up and he smacked the table lightly with his palm. "Oh," he cried, "I think I understand."

Krystal waited smilingly for him to share his new understanding.

"You serve the salad first over here, don't you?"

Krystal arched her eyebrows again and poked her head slightly forward.

"And the main course isn't served until the salad's completed, right?"

She responded with a tiny nod.

"In England," he went on, "restaurants only serve the salad as a side order *with* the main meal." He lifted his salad plate and set it down in front of him. "Hah!" he cried, reaching for his fork. "I might have been waiting a long time for my meal tonight, eh?"

Krystal laughed softly. Brad winked at her and began rapidly forking his salad into his mouth.

• • • • •

The snake-bird Mallus flicked his forked tongue at Ratsbane. "You are familiar with the Prime-Evil Impulse Transducer?"

Ratsbane straightened his wart-covered back and poked his nose in the air. "I was foreman of Subsector 477 before coming here!" he boasted.

"Yes," Mallus answered. "I know that. But aren't you the one who couldn't break the Powerlink of those commandos at Eisenhower High?"

"I did break their Powerlink!" Ratsbane shrieked. His bulbous black eyes glared at Mallus. He prepared to protest Mallus's attack on his ability when the foreman waved a feathery wing in his face.

"No matter," he announced perfunctorily. "I will train you well enough, no matter what your past record has been." He turned to face the console of computer screens. "Your primary directive in Subsector 477 was breaking the Powerlink by preventing prayer, right?" he asked.

Ratsbane nodded.

"Like Subsector 477, we have to prevent any purposeful prayer here too!" Mallus began to speak slowly to punctuate his every word. "Because it is purposeful prayer that connects them to their power source—our Enemy."

A chill went down Ratsbane's ugly spine. Mallus continued, "But *our* prime directive here in Subsector 1122 is not to initially break the Powerlink, it is to implement a two-pronged strategy that will *keep it broken*."

"Which is . . . ?" prompted Ratsbane.

"There will be time for that later," Mallus answered. "Right now, we both have urgent duties to attend to." Mallus stared again at the monitor focused on Krystal Wayne. "Here," he said, pointing a feather at the screen. "Get a headset and let me see how well you work the keyboard."

Ratsbane grabbed a headset from a hook on the console and clamped it over his shiny head.

"Back up that view," Mallus instructed. "I want to see the rest of that room in the restaurant. Can you do that?"

Ratsbane didn't answer but hunched his shoulders over the PIT keyboard and spat sharp commands into his headset microphone. Within a few moments, the view on the screen widened and Krystal became a small form in the corner of the room.

Mallus pointed his scaly head toward the monitor and peered at the picture. "Ah!" he blurted finally. "There! On the wall!" He kept the tip of a feather trained on the screen while Ratsbane worked the keyboard, finally managing to zero in on the object of Mallus's attention.

"A thermostat," Mallus said. The narrow slits of his eyes searched the screen once more, and his tongue flicked nervously in and out of his mouth. "Oh, hallelujah!" He clapped the end of a wing over his mouth and glared in horror at Ratsbane. He spun his serpent head around to see if any of the demons in the area had heard his exclamation. Then he turned and cuffed Ratsbane with a mighty swipe of his wing, sending the toad-ant reeling into the metal railing that surrounded the PIT platform.

Before Ratsbane could move, Mallus pounced on him again, snatched his toad body with both hands, and hurled him back against the PIT console. He backed Ratsbane against the wall of computer screens and croaked menacingly in his face, "You never heard that, did you, my little toad-ant? I never said what you thought I said. Do you understand?"

Ratsbane nodded fearfully. Mallus spun him around to face the screen once more and pointed with a primary feather.

"There. Next to the kitchen door. You see that man in the suit? He must be the manager or owner or something." He moved his feather slightly. "See, he's standing right next to the thermostat. Hit him with a few impulses; suggest to him that he feels a chill, that his customers are cold. If we can get him to turn up the heat, maybe *we* can turn it up too."

Ratsbane turned his head and grinned at Mallus. "I see what you're doing, fanning the flames of love."

Mallus whacked the back of Ratsbane's head. "You imbecile! This isn't about love. It's about sex!" His voice began to get louder with each word. "What are you, Ratsbane, a new recruit? There's not a demon in hell who wants people—especially these repulsive teenagers—to experience true love. Love is a strategy of the Enemy, and it doesn't do a thing for hell. We counterfeit it, yes. We make other things *look* like love, and we use those counterfeits to tell people that it's okay to have sex outside of the Enemy's plan. But the only thing we *love* is hate!"

Mallus stopped shouting and took a deep breath. He pointed again at the flickering monitor. "If we can get that restaurant hot enough to get her to take her sweater off, that's one less obstacle in Romeo's way. I don't want them to fall into love; I want them to fall into the sack!"

• • • • •

Krystal ran a finger along the curve of her turtleneck. *I guess I dressed too warm tonight,* she thought. *Still, this date is turning out a lot nicer than I expected.* She curled a final forkful of linguine and smiled at Brad. Her initial irritation at him for not warning her to dress appropriately had faded; he'd been a charming date through the entire meal.

"I've told you some things that I don't think my closest friends even know," she said in answer to Brad's latest question about her. "I feel like all we've talked about all night long is me. Why don't you tell me some things about you?"

"Ah. Well," he said, clipping each syllable short. "All right. Let's see. I'm from Derby, England." He pronounced it "Darby." "That's in Derbyshire. My father's an engineer for Rolls Royce. He's working at the aircraft plant in Hogan."

"Is that near London? Derby, I mean."

"About 135 miles north of the capital, I guess. Derby is right in the center of England. It's called the Midlands."

"Do you have a girlfriend? In Derby?" The moment it was out of her mouth, Krystal was embarrassed that she had asked it. *You sound like you're interested in applying for the position,* she scolded herself.

"No. I never knew a girl who could hold my attention for very long," he said. He looked meaningfully at Krystal. "In Derby," he added.

Brad held Krystal's chair as they left the table. As the night air chilled her, she recalled how warm the restaurant had been and thought that maybe it reflected her feelings about Brad. *He turned me off at first,* she admitted. *But he's been such a gentleman and has made me feel so grown up tonight.*

The way he opened doors for her and ordered the meal and paid the check at the restaurant made him seem much older, more mature than any boy she had ever dated, she thought.

He makes me feel like the only girl in the world.

* * * * * *

Mallus glowered at the beaming bank of monitors on the PIT console. "That female is impossible!" he said. "How could she keep her sweater on in that heat?"

"It's not all bad, Foreman Mallus," Ratsbane suggested.

"Look at this." He typed in a few commands and leaned back from the keyboard. A picture appeared on the screen of two paramedics rolling a stretcher out of the restaurant. "This old lady at the very next table succumbed to the heat and fainted. She has a heart condition."

"Go jump in the Lake of Fire, you dimwit. I don't give a sniff of sulfur for that old lady. We've got a job to do, do you hear me?" Mallus smacked Ratsbane on the top of his smooth, round ant head. "Where are they now?" he asked. "What's happening?"

Ratsbane called up the images of Brad and Krystal in Brad's car.

"Hellfire!" Mallus groaned.

"What?" Ratsbane asked. He looked at the screen, then turned his gaze on Mallus again. "What's wrong now?"

"Bucket seats! Romeo's got bucket seats. Oh, I'm going to have to file a written complaint on this one. Why don't we just put a few cactus plants between these two. That wouldn't be any worse!"

Ratsbane watched as Brad pulled the car to a stop in a clearing beside a country road well outside of Westcastle.

* * * * *

Krystal's discomfort was visible as Brad turned the car off and they sat in the darkness in a small clearing surrounded almost completely by trees.

"What are we doing here?" she asked.

"Relax, Krystal. You're going to like this."

Her uneasiness increased. She didn't like the way things looked, and she didn't like the way things sounded.

"I don't want to stay here, Brad," she said firmly.

"It won't take long, Krystal. Just don't make any noise."

THE EDUCATION
OF BRAD STUART

P anic gripped Krystal and she fumbled frantically for the door handle. Brad reached out a strong arm and grasped her wrist.

"Shhh!" he said.

She was torn between wrenching her arm free and opening the door.

"Now!" he whispered, and flipped on the headlights of the car. Krystal froze and stared at two deer, spotlighted in the light, not more than fifteen yards from the car. The deer stood perfectly still, mesmerized by the lights. Krystal dropped her hand from the car door. Brad still held her wrist.

"Aren't they magnificent?" he said.

"They're beautiful," she answered, sighed deeply and leaned back into the bucket seat. *Take it easy, Krystal,* she told herself. *You're letting your imagination run away with you.* She glanced at Brad, who sat still, bewitched by the deer. *You've obviously misjudged him,* she scolded herself.

A few moments later, as they sat still wordlessly watching the deer, Krystal shifted and leaned her head very lightly on Brad's shoulder.

●　●　●　●　●

"I thought we had her there for a minute," Ratsbane confided to Mallus.

"Idiot," Mallus said, though he, too, had watched the action between Brad and Krystal with hope. "That's far too clumsy for my taste."

The two demons lapsed into silence as they viewed the couple in the car. Ratsbane finally broke the quiet.

"You want me to see if I can get some impulses through to the 'spud'?"

"You mean 'stud,' you fool."

"Right," Ratsbane said. He inspected the screen and began typing as Mallus dictated strategy.

"Yeah, that's good," Mallus said. "That's good. She's got her head on his shoulder. Okay, Romeo, you want to get her horizontal as soon as possible. Good, good. Arm around her shoulder. Great!"

Ratsbane typed furiously and snarled commands into the microphone. The couple on the screen began exchanging kisses.

"Ahhh," Mallus hissed. "She's melting. He's good, all right." He watched, tapping a bird foot and flicking his tongue in and out. "Okay, Ratsbane, tell him to go for the bra strap now."

Ratsbane bent over his work. Mallus watched the action in the car.

"Good, uh huh," Mallus said, as Brad's hand rubbed Krystal's back. He embraced her tightly, moving both hands caressingly over her back.

"What are you waiting for?" Mallus grumbled at the screen.

"I'm doing the best I can," Ratsbane answered.

"It's not good enough. Go for the bra!" He was shouting again. "You won't get anywhere as long as she's encased in all those layers of clothing."

Mallus's shouting and cursing continued as Brad and Krystal embraced and kissed without any apparent move in the direction Ratsbane was suggesting through the PIT waves.

"It's not going to happen, your malevolence." Ratsbane sighed as Brad reached for the key to start the car.

Mallus shouted a string of obscenities and slapped the back of Ratsbane's head.

"I think he was—" Ratsbane rubbed the smooth surface of his head, then continued, "I think he was a little discouraged from making any move by her, uh, by what she wore, sir."

"You incompetent! I've gotten male subjects through more layers of clothing than a mummy in a coffin! It's not him, you sorry excuse for a demon, it's you!" Mallus stormed away.

Ratsbane spat a red wad onto the floor as he watched Mallus stalk off the PIT platform and onto the floor of the cavern.

* * * * *

Brad gripped Krystal's waist tightly as he walked her to the door of the Davis residence.

As she prepared to say good night, Krystal felt as though a balloon filled with warm water had settled in her chest. It felt wonderful and just a little uncomfortable at the same time.

"I had a nice time tonight, Brad," she said, purposely trying not to sound too enthusiastic.

He grinned, and the hue of his blue eyes seemed to reflect all the depth of the night sky. Krystal closed her eyes, expecting to be kissed any moment.

"May I knock you up next Friday?"

The balloon in Krystal's chest burst suddenly and she felt it plop rudely into her stomach. Her eyes popped wide open.

What did he say? she thought. Brad stood before her, blinking innocently it seemed. *Did I hear him right?* Panic gripped her now where the warm balloon used to be. She prepared to rebuff him and march into the house when he said, "Are you all right, Krystal?"

"You—" She swallowed. "What did you say?"

His eyebrows made themselves into little tents above his eyes. "Did I say something wrong? Is it too forward to ask you out again next Friday?"

"I thought you said—" She stopped. She wasn't going to say it. She couldn't.

"What? What I said was, em, 'I wonder if I could knock you up, em, next Friday.' Is there something wrong?"

"You—you don't see anything wrong with that?"

Brad looked piercingly at her. "I'm afraid there's something I'm not getting."

Krystal's face reddened, and she looked away from Brad's eyes. "'Knock you up,'" she said, then cleared her throat, "means to, uh, get a girl pregnant."

Brad blinked again, several times, then burst into hooting laughter.

Krystal turned her head back to the house, sure that Mrs. Davis could hear Brad all the way upstairs.

"What's so funny?" she snapped. "I don't think it's funny."

Brad struggled to control himself. Even in the porch light, his face was purple with pleasure. "I'm sorry," he said between hoots. "I had no idea." He paused to catch his breath. "I had no idea," he repeated and began laughing louder than ever.

Krystal stiffened. *How could he think that wouldn't offend me?* The balloon inside her slipped still lower as she considered the possibility that Brad might have already heard the gossip about what she had been like before she became a Christian, how she had been one of the wildest students at Ike, a drug user, sexually active since the eighth grade. Shame for her former behavior—which she had struggled with even since becoming a Christian—rose in her again. *Maybe that's why he asked me out in the first place,* she thought, *because he'd heard what I used to be like.* All her anger and indignation at Brad began to fade as her self-esteem plunged.

Brad recovered himself, inhaled deeply and, with a smile that gleamed in the porch light, spoke soothingly to Krystal.

"I apologize for the misunderstanding," he said and swallowed another giggle. "I had no idea what I was saying. You see, where I come from, 'May I knock you up next Friday' is an old expression meaning, 'May I come to your house and call for you?'" He motioned with his fist as though he were knocking on a door. "I did not mean to imply anything indecent. I'm still learning the language."

Krystal stared wide-eyed at him like the deer they had seen in the clearing earlier that night, a flood of contradictory emotions wrestling inside her.

Brad smiled warmly again and wrapped his arms around her. He pulled her face close to his. "May I 'take you out' next Friday evening, Krystal Wayne?" Their eyes were bare inches apart. "Did I say that right?"

Krystal closed her eyes in answer, and they kissed, long.

* * * * *

Krystal breezed into Mr. Detweiler's office, a closet of a room jammed with a desk, a chair, and one bookcase. Books, papers, and overstuffed file folders covered every available surface in the cubicle.

"Am I the first one here?" she asked just before noticing that Mr. Detweiler cradled the telephone receiver between his shoulder and ear. She mouthed the word, "Sorry," and shrugged her shoulders. He motioned her into the classroom beyond the little office with a nod of his head.

As Mr. Detweiler talked on the phone, others joined Krystal: Stanley, the talkative freshman who always carried a bag full of books; Chase Everett, Mr. Detweiler's "pet" on the debate team; Leeann, the blonde who always seemed to wear a dozen layers of clothing; Jason Withers; and a few others.

Each student entered the classroom differently, some shuffling, some nearly skipping. But once inside, all assumed a businesslike air, as if they had been summoned into the Oval Office to brief the president.

Krystal watched Jason slip quietly into the room and circle behind the others. He casually picked up Stanley's book bag and strolled over to where Leeann had set down her bag.

I never noticed that they carried the same book bag, she thought, then smiled. *But Jason obviously did.*

Jason set Stanley's bag beside Leeann's, then lifted hers and walked back to place it where Stanley's had been. The switch was accomplished in seconds. Jason never cracked a smile. He never glanced at another person in the room except when Krystal caught his eye; then he winked at her. He accomplished his task with the nonchalance of a boy kicking a can down a deserted street.

"Do you forgive me for the other night?" Brad had approached Krystal from behind and placed a hand on her shoulder.

"Forgive you? For what?" she asked, quickly blushing as she remembered the answer to her own question. "Oh, yeah," she said softly. She flashed a shy smile.

"I know that I've a lot to learn yet," he told her. "I *am* learning to speak 'American,' though. I don't ask my teachers if I can go to the loo anymore."

"The what?"

"The loo." He laughed, not the hooting laugh as before, but a warm, easy chuckle. "They all look at me funny too—just like you're doing right now." He winked at her. "Back home in England that's what we call restrooms."

Krystal screwed up her face to reflect her confusion. "The loo? Why do you call it *that?*"

"Well, why do you call it a *bathroom?* You Americans raise your hand, the teacher calls on you, and you say, 'May I please go to the *bath*room?'" He mimicked a high-pitched female voice. "I defy you to show me a bathtub in any of the *loos* in the entire school! You *can't!* There are only toilets, no baths!"

"Shhh!" she admonished, and her warning gave way to a musical giggle.

"And 'restroom' is no better! I don't see many people resting in there. Maybe it's different in the ladies' room?"

Others had been listening to Brad's impassioned speech. "I can see why you're on the debate team," Krystal whispered.

"Well, I hope you had a good time last Friday."

"Oh, I did. How—" She stopped herself, afraid that she was talking too fast again and too excitedly. "How did you know the deer would be there?"

"I didn't. A friend of my father, a fellow named Ted, was telling us the other night that he takes his kiddies out there occasionally. I thought it might be, em, rather romantic."

Krystal nearly blurted, "Oh, it was!" but Mr. Detweiler entered the room and cleared his throat with an air of authority. She slid into the seat next to Jason, and Brad returned to his former seat at the back of the room.

"What *is* it with you and James Bond?" Jason asked.

"What?" she said defensively. "Nothing, okay?"

"He's paying an awful lot of attention to you. Tell me," he continued as Mr. Detweiler shot a few glances in their direction, "does his Aston Martin have an ejection seat?"

"What?" she asked. Then, getting his joke, added, "Stop!"

"I just think it's only fair to warn you that if you tug on his ear, his head inflates into a big yellow lifeboat."

"Miss Wayne." Mr. Detweiler spoke sternly and loudly. "Is there a problem?"

"No, sir," she answered. She glanced at Jason, who was holding his nose. It was reddening from the light backhand smack Krystal had just applied to it.

"I want you all to understand," Mr. Detweiler said, "that forensics is unlike any other extracurricular pursuit in this school. In fact, I like to refer to it as cocurricular instead of extracurricular because, unlike the football team or the tennis team, forensics reinforces and applies the education you receive in your classes. It requires long hours, it requires intellectual exertion, and it requires"—he shot another look in Krystal and Jason's direction—"mature behavior. But you'll be rewarded. Many times over, I assure you.

"Now," Detweiler continued, "let's begin with the two areas of forensics: debate and I.E.

"In debate, you're assigned a topic—"

Brad Stuart raised his hand into the air without lifting his elbow from the desk. Mr. Detweiler saw the movement and nodded.

"It's *always* an assigned topic?"

"Yes," Mr. Detweiler answered.

"Em, for example, what might a typical subject be?"

"Oh, examples of novice questions—there are three levels in debate: novice, junior varsity, and varsity—a novice might debate on the subject 'Coal consumption in China,' or 'Women's development in third world countries.'"

Brad stared back at Mr. Detweiler. After a pause, he said, "You're joking."

"No, Mr. Stuart," he replied with an offended tone, "I am not joking."

"I don't mean to be rude," Brad said, "but are the assigned subjects ever relevant?"

"Relevant? To whom?"

"To me." He glanced around the room. "To all of us. I mean to say, it's good, I'm sure, to address the subject of coal consumption in developing countries, but wouldn't it be more interesting and beneficial to debate on topics like I proposed the other day? The distribution of condoms in public schools, for example?"

"What *is* it," Jason Withers interposed, "with you and condoms? Do you own stock in a condom company or something?" Several students snickered, but Jason wasn't joking this time. His expression was serious.

Brad blinked at Jason as though he had never seen him before.

"Nothing," he answered, "nothing at all. I've just been rather surprised at how backward you Americans are on the subject." Every head in the room pointed Brad's direction, but no one spoke. "Back home, it's understood that people our age are going to have sex; it's a fact of life and it's no good sweeping it under the carpet."

Jason opened his mouth but closed it again before speaking.

"I say that the responsible thing to do, since teenagers are having sex anyway, is to protect them, to teach them how to protect themselves."

"By passing out condoms in homeroom?" Jason's question dripped with sarcasm.

"Yes," Brad answered emphatically. "And by showing the proper way to use a condom."

"And I suppose you'll volunteer for the demonstration, right?"

"Look," Brad continued in a subdued voice. "Which would you prefer, for your sister to practice safe sex, or have her get AIDS?"

Krystal watched the exchange between the two like a spectator at a tennis match. She sat helplessly by while her friend, Jason, got madder and madder at Brad, her—*well what is he, anyway?* she thought. *He's not your boyfriend,* she told herself. *You've only gone out once.* Distracted by the debate between Brad and Jason, she couldn't decide how to complete her thought. *So maybe he's not a boyfriend yet,* she figured. *But he's something. That's for sure. He's something.*

Krystal rode with Darcelle to Duane and Liz Cunningham's apartment.

Duane and Liz had become youth leaders at Westcastle Community Church about a year ago, as the Liberation Commandos were just beginning their campaign to bring about the deliverance of their school friends from Satan's control. The group had changed a lot since last fall. Buster Todd and Darcelle Davis, Amber, Will, Jason, and Joy were there, of course. Tony Ortiz, who had been dating Amber Lockwood at this time last year, was a freshman on scholarship at State University; Reggie Spencer, one of Krystal's former boyfriends, had graduated last spring and was now working on Duane's construction crew, though he remained one of the most enthusiastic and effective commandos.

There had been some additions too: Krystal, who had become a Christian through the group; Marci Small, who had come to Christ and the Liberation Commandos through Jason Withers; Hillary Putnam and the two other rally team members she and Amber had led to Christ, Kim Holmes and Debi White.

Janice Hurley, though she attended another church, met with the group too.

As Duane began the meeting, each person said a few words about their successes and failures in the Christian life during the past week and requested prayer for their non-believing friends.

Krystal pursed her lips when her turn came. She hesitated a moment before starting.

"Okay. This has been a really confusing week for me."

She looked around at everyone in the circle. When she met Jason's gaze, he crossed his eyes at her. She smiled.

"I guess you all know a little about me and my sister, Kathy. Well, she told me she's getting married next June." She picked up her dainty necklace and began turning it over between her fingers. "She asked me to be in her wedding." She screwed up her face again. "I, uh, I guess I should be happy about that, but, I don't know . . . I don't know how I feel.

"And," she continued, "I went out last Friday with Brad Stuart, the new boy at school from England." Her voice rose as if she were asking a question. The others in the circle nodded to indicate they knew who she meant. "Well, he's not a Christian and, I mean, it went really well, I guess, but . . ." She exhaled loudly and released the necklace from her grasp. "I guess I don't know how to feel about that either."

Liz spoke first, after a long silence.

"How do you know he's not a Christian?" she asked.

Krystal snapped her eyes over to Jason. They both smiled. "I know," she answered with a hint of a giggle.

"Does this boy know *you're* a Christian?" Liz countered.

Krystal glanced from Liz to several others in the room, but she wasn't thinking about them. She was searching her mind and memory for an answer to Liz's question.

"Yeah, I think so." She noticed, as everyone else in the room did, that there was a note of surprise in her voice. "I mean, I prayed for my food in the restaurant and he started telling me how Americans are more open about their religion than they are in England. We didn't really talk about it that much. He may think I'm just 'religious,' since we didn't really discuss anything about my being a Christian."

Krystal caught Liz and Duane exchanging a glance, and Duane spoke next. "Maybe that's a goal. Maybe this week you could try to find a way to share your faith with him and let him know where you stand."

When the last person in the group had spoken, they bowed their heads—a couple of people folded their hands or even knelt beside their chair—and prayed for the things that had been mentioned. Amber Lockwood, who was sitting to Krystal's right, prayed for her. As Amber mentioned Kathy's wedding and Krystal's feelings for her sister and then went on to pray for Brad, Krystal realized she hadn't prayed about either subject until that moment.

As Amber prayed, however, Krystal felt overwhelmed by the way she felt the group had reacted to her relationship with Brad. *These are my friends,* she thought. *Why do I feel like they're all looking at me funny? I feel like they're judging me, like I'm doing something wrong.*

She tried to dismiss the nagging thoughts from her mind

and concentrate on praying with the others in the group, but she felt like she'd somehow lost the ability to pray, like a student blanking out on a big test.

"Krystal, honey, the phone. It's for you." Mom Davis's head disappeared behind the door of Krystal's room, where it had appeared seconds earlier.

Krystal rubbed her eyes and looked at the digits on her clock radio: 11:57. *Who would call me this late?* she wondered.

She picked up the receiver and held it to her ear. She whispered a hoarse, "Hello?"

"Krystal! It's me, Jason."

"Jason. What's wrong? Is everything all right? Are you okay?"

"Krystal, I forgot all about it."

"What? Forgot about what?"

"The bags. I forgot to tell Stanley and Leeann that I switched their book bags! I meant to tell them if they didn't discover it before the meeting let out, but I got all bent out of shape because of that—" He stopped abruptly. Krystal knew why. "Because of my argument with Brad," he finished.

"It's after midnight now, Jason. There's not much you can do about it until tomorrow."

"I guess you're right." He paused. "Krystal?"

She answered with a "hmm?" pronounced behind closed lips.

"Are you still going to go out with that guy?"

She thought she knew Jason's reasons for asking the question: Brad's conceited, he's not a Christian, and he seems to have some pretty wild ideas. *But he's not like that when he's with me,* she wanted to say. *He's different.* She realized suddenly why she'd been in such an odd mood since the meeting at Duane and Liz's house.

"Jason?" She breathed his name to make sure she had his attention, then continued without waiting for him to respond. "I've never felt this way before."

Silence hung between the two friends for a few long moments, until Jason finally spoke.

"I'm sorry I woke you up," he said. "Good night, Krystal."

FALLING IN
AND OUT OF LOVE

Krystal gripped the handle of the screen door without turning it.

You should talk to her, Darcelle had said. *Tell your sister the things you've told me. Just be honest about the way you feel.*

Now she stood again at the back door of the house and summoned the courage to go in. She opened the door and tiptoed in, careful not to make any noise. She paused inside the door and listened. Voices came from the dining room—female voices.

She stole across the kitchen and listened at the swinging door that led to the dining room.

"You still have plenty of time to decide, sweetheart."

Krystal recognized her mother's voice. She leaned on the swinging door and held it slightly ajar.

"But he's always been so good to me. He's never—"

The other voice belonged to her sister Kathy, who had started sniffling and blew her nose. She sniffed and started again.

"How am I supposed to know, Mom? How can I ever be sure? I don't want to mess up my whole life."

"I know, sweetheart," her mother said.

"How did you know you wanted to marry Dad?"

Krystal listened. There was a long pause. Krystal worried that they suspected her presence and were looking her way, waiting for her to show herself. Finally her mom spoke, with a voice that quivered.

"I've never told you this before, sweetheart. But if you want me to be honest . . ." She paused again. "I don't know if my decision to marry your father was the right decision or not."

The room fell silent. A tickle rose in Krystal's throat, but she stifled the urge to cough.

"At the time," she said, "I thought we were made for each other. But in a lot of ways, I was still a little girl, very naive. There were a lot of things I didn't know."

Krystal couldn't hear her sister's whispered question, but her mother answered, "I don't know that any more than you do, Kathy. Moms don't have all the answers, you know."

"Yeah," Kathy whispered. Then, after another long pause, she spoke again, with a flatness in her voice that chilled Krystal. "It wouldn't be a bad thing for me to marry Bill. We get along well together."

"You make it sound like a death sentence."

"I do? Yeah, I guess I do. I mean, he's a great guy, but —" She stopped. "I don't know, I just don't know if he's the one."

"Kathy, why do you feel such pressure to make that decision now? Why can't you just give it more time? It's better to put off a wedding too long than it is to not put it off long enough."

Krystal didn't stay to hear her sister's response. She eased the door back into its place and retraced her steps across the kitchen and out the back door.

"Krystal!" Janice pulled Krystal aside the next day between third and fourth period. "Did you hear what your boyfriend did?"

Krystal clucked her tongue. "He's not my boyfriend," she insisted.

"You knew who I was talking about, though, didn't you?" Janice said teasingly.

Krystal twisted her lips into a scornful grimace.

"Anyway," Janice persisted, "I heard that Brad went up to Brenda McCain—she's in his first-period class—and asked her for a *rubber!* Just like that, as if there was nothing to it. 'May I please borrow a rubber?' he said. Can you believe it?" She shuddered with revulsion.

"I don't believe it," Krystal said.

"It's all over school. Everybody's talking about it."

Jason Withers rolled around the corner by the two girls and nearly scattered them like bowling pins. "Did you hear?" he started.

"Yes," Janice gasped, "but Krystal won't believe it."

"Believe it," Jason said, panting. "You know he has some fixation about condoms. I'm telling you, Krystal, the guy's a scuzball. Give him his walking papers."

Krystal crossed her arms stubbornly.

"Ditch him," he urged. "Give him the ol' heave-ho, send him packing, throw him over, show him the door, give him a one-way ticket back to England."

"He's not my boyfriend. But I wish you would give him a chance. He's not the ogre you two seem to think he is."

"Ogre at two o'clock," Jason hissed. The girls looked up just as Brad arrived and draped a familiar arm across Krystal's shoulders.

Brad smiled engagingly at the trio. Krystal blushed and shrunk slightly from the weight of Brad's arm, but he didn't remove it.

"Did I interrupt something?" Brad asked, sensing the discomfort of Krystal and her friends.

Jason and Janice glanced at Krystal simultaneously. Their gazes dropped to the floor and the question hung, unanswered.

Krystal finally broke the awkward silence. "People are saying—" she shot a defiant glance at Jason—"that you asked Brenda McCain for a rubber this morning." She blushed a shade deeper.

He nodded agreeably. "Oh, yes," he admitted and then began chuckling.

Krystal shook his arm off her shoulders and turned to face him fully. He looked back at her good-naturedly.

"I told her I'd give it back as soon as I was finished with it," he explained cheerfully.

Laughter began to rise in him, and the others recognized that Brad was trying not to laugh now. "She gasped and gagged as if she'd swallowed a grapefruit," he said. Janice, Jason, and Krystal stared at the snickering boy with the refined accent. He gathered his laughter back into his mouth and forced it back down his throat.

"You think it's funny?" Jason demanded, holding his arms tightly against his body, his hands balled into fists.

"Oh, okay. Take it easy. I'm just having a little fun with you. It was totally innocent, I assure you," he said. "You see, in England, a rubber is what you call, em, an eraser! I only wanted to correct a mistake I'd made. I tried to apologize but I'm afraid she was unconvinced. She wouldn't—" He paused to allow himself a tight smirk. "She wouldn't allow me near her to explain myself."

"So," Krystal said, "this was all about an . . . an eraser?" Her voice signaled her relief.

Brad turned his palms up in the air to indicate helplessness. Krystal faced her friends smugly. Jason rolled his eyes at Janice and they walked away together.

"Don't worry, Brad," Krystal said as she hugged his arm tightly. "They'll accept you." He looked at her doubtfully and she added, "Sooner or later."

Krystal met Darcelle after school at their usual spot.

"You ready?" Darcelle asked when Krystal failed to fall into step beside her to walk to the car. The clear afternoon wind whipped around the corners of the school building and jingled the cords on the flagpole.

"You go ahead," Krystal said, pitching her head the direction of the parking lot. "I'm meeting someone. I'll be along later."

"Brad?" Darcelle asked.

"Huh?" Krystal responded, then belatedly realized she'd heard Darcelle perfectly. "Oh, yeah," she admitted.

"You know, Krystal," Darcelle began as she reversed her direction and stopped to face her friend, "we haven't really talked much recently. I guess I've been kind of waiting for the right opportunity to talk to you about Brad."

Krystal said nothing. Her cheeks met the chill breeze with a pink blush.

"I guess I was kind of hoping, well, you know, that you two wouldn't really get very serious, but it kind of seems like you're getting along pretty well, right?"

Krystal shrugged.

Darcelle breathed deeply. "Look, if it's none of my business, I'm sorry, but I'm kind of concerned. The Bible says not to be 'unequally yoked' with unbelievers and, well, your relationship with Brad seems to fit into that category."

"Dar," Krystal said, calling her by the nickname only Darcelle's family used, "I appreciate your concern, but I don't think you and Jason and the others have even given Brad a chance." The blush on her cheeks deepened. "I know him;

you don't. I wish you would spend as much time trying to be a friend to him as you do criticizing him."

Darcelle held a hand up in surrender. "Krystal, I'm really not—"

"Here he comes now," Krystal interrupted, signaling Brad's approach with her gleaming eyes. She wiggled her fingers at Darcelle and took Brad's arm in hers. They walked arm in arm to the school lot, leaving Darcelle staring after them and listening to the *chink* of the flagpole cord beating its rhythm in the wind.

Krystal inhaled deeply through her nose. Her face was inches from Brad's and she tried to guess the fragrance he wore.

They sat across a square library table from each other. Books and papers—which they had not consulted since sitting down—covered the surface in front of them. A leafy green plant, which they had removed from the center of the table to make room for their school materials, sat alone on the floor beside them. The afternoon sunlight knifed through the narrow windows behind Brad and striped a light and dark pattern on the floor and furniture.

"Is it *Fixation?*" she attempted.

"Beg your pardon?" he said in his rich accent.

"The cologne you're wearing. Is it *Fixation?*"

"Oh, I don't know," he said, shrugging the question off. "Something I brought with me from home. From England."

"Oh," she said. "Tell me more about England. About yourself. What's your favorite singing group?"

He grinned. "You've never heard of them, I'm sure."

"Who are they?"

"Well," he said. "At least we're not eating."

"Why do you say that?"

"My favorite singing group. It's a band called 'Toe Jam.'"

"Toe Jam?" she echoed.

He nodded and chuckled heartily.

They laughed together, then, and he put his arm around her. They kissed.

"I think your accent is very romantic," she whispered in a throaty voice.

"I'm not the one with an accent," he answered, and they laughed again.

"Tell me something else," she said.

"Something else?"

"About England. About ways we're different."

"Well, em, let me see. When you go out to eat, you get fries with your meal, right?" Krystal nodded. "We don't. We order chips."

"Like potato chips?"

He shook his head fervently. "No, they're much the same as what you call fries, but thicker. And we eat them with practically everything."

She smiled. "What else?"

"More? All right, em, well, everything on this side of the pond is much larger, on a much grander scale. You see, because England is an island, space is at a premium—space to build even more so. So everything back home is rather small and compact.

"In the States, you still have more space than you need, so you make everything so much larger than it has to be, extravagantly large."

"What are the girls like over there?"

He leaned close, until their lips nearly touched. "Not one of them compares to you."

Krystal caught her breath.

"How long," she said when she had wrestled her emotions under control, "how long is your family supposed to be staying over here?"

"Em, my father is here on a limited work visa."

"So what's that mean?"

"Probably a year."

She rolled her necklace between her fingers as she pondered his answer. "That's not very long, is it?"

A chubby blond boy with a crew cut barreled around the corner and rammed their table with his belly. He groaned and staggered off, holding his paunch, just a few paces ahead of the girl pursuing him.

"I hope to stay longer," Brad said, paralyzing Krystal with his deep blue eyes. "Or to come back. Maybe for university."

She smiled and lowered her gaze. "I'd like that," she said quietly.

Brad drove Krystal home from the library. She knew she was late for dinner, but that mattered very little to her.

Brad parked at the curb in front of the Davis home, and the conversation began to dwindle. He leaned over between the bucket seats, touched her cheek lightly with his hand, and kissed her.

Before she knew it, they were in each other's arms, becoming more and more involved physically. It was not yet dark outside, and Krystal imagined that Darcelle or Mom Davis might see them making out through the windows of the house. Still, she felt completely uninhibited. Her feelings for Brad were so strong that she just wanted to be closer to him.

It was Brad who finally broke their embrace. "Um," he said, clearing his throat and returning his hands to the steering wheel. "I think we ought to stop." He glanced toward the house and its large picture window. "They may be waiting dinner for you."

Krystal drew a sharp breath, strangely relieved and disappointed at the same time. "Yeah, I guess," she said, dropping her gaze. "Good night," she said. She placed a hand on the handle and, leaning back toward Brad, kissed him and got out.

Krystal said little as Mrs. Davis warmed a plate of food in the microwave oven for her. Although she had done nothing with Brad that they had not done before, she felt scared and ashamed.

What was I doing? she wondered. *I was way out of control. If he hadn't stopped when he did, I would've—I would've kept going! Right in front of the house! And I'm the one who's supposed to be a Christian!*

She ate her food in silence, only speaking to respond to Mom Davis or answer one of her questions. The rest of the time, Krystal thought and worried. *What am I going to do? If*

being with him makes me lose my head . . . but I can't stop
seeing him. What am I going to do?

She closed herself in her room for the rest of the night and
went to bed early, still troubled by the question, *What am I*
going to do?

STALLED BY THE SIDE OF THE ROAD

Darcelle entered Duane and Liz Cunningham's apartment alone. Most of the Liberation Commandos already crowded the living room, which seemed to get smaller with each meeting.

Jason sat on the floor, next to the couch, which was shared by Will, Amber, and Joy. Darcelle lowered herself onto the floor next to Jason and crossed her legs.

"Is Krystal coming?" Jason asked Darcelle.

She shook her head.

"Where is she?" he pressed.

She shrugged. "She said something about having to think some things through."

Duane started the meeting, interrupting Jason's interrogation of Darcelle. But though Jason watched and listened as the meeting progressed and tried hard to concentrate during the prayer time, Krystal occupied his mind every moment.

When the meeting was over and most of the group were just hanging around talking, Jason slapped Will on the knee. "Meet me in the kitchen," he said in a low voice.

Jason breezed through the swinging door and into the kitchen, nearly running into Liz and Hillary, who cut their conversation off abruptly.

"Sorry," he sang, and in one smooth motion, performed a pirouette and followed the swinging door on its return journey out of the kitchen.

"That's no good," he told Will, who stopped suddenly to avoid colliding with Jason on his surprise exit from the kitchen. "Come on."

The two friends finally found momentary privacy in the stairwell of the apartment building, just outside Liz and Duane's apartment.

"What's up?" Will asked as he and Jason sat, shoulder touching shoulder, on the top step.

Jason made several false starts, and finally said, "You know I clown around a lot. But I'm starting to wish I was a more serious kind of person." He let out a long sigh, and they sat in silence for a few moments. When he spoke again, it was in slow, measured syllables. "I guess I want to know how I can get people to take me seriously."

"How you can get people to take you seriously?" Will echoed.

"Yeah," Jason said, then considered. "Well, girls, I guess. How can I get girls to take me seriously?"

It was Will's turn to sigh. "I don't know, Jason," he said. "Why are you asking me?"

"How did you get Amber to take you seriously? Especially after you lost your shorts in the lake?"

If it had been a less intense conversation, the two friends might have broken out in laughter. They only smiled at each other.

"I don't know," Will repeated. Jason sat quietly, aware that Will was honestly trying to remember, to be helpful to his friend. "I guess it was when we started working together, you know, when we first started praying and sharing our faith with Tony and Marlon."

Jason stared at Will as the wheels turned in his mind.

Brad grasped Krystal's hand as they wound through the crowd exiting the stadium.

"How do you know so much about pro football?" she asked Brad. It was a mild fall Sunday afternoon; Krystal wore a coat, but Brad now carried his jacket. "I thought they only played soccer over in England."

"Americans!" he said, rolling his eyes in mock anger. "You think that just because you're isolated from the rest of the world, everyone else is too." He narrowly avoided a collision with a large man carrying a walkie-talkie. He let go of Krystal's hand, maneuvered around the man, and snatched her hand into his once more. "American football has become very big back home. Oh, most Brits did not recognize American football as a 'proper' game until recently, but that's been changing fairly quickly. My chums and I saw the Bears and the Giants in an exhibition game last year."

"Oh," she said, smiling at his accent and his use of the word "chums." She still loved to hear him speak; during the couple of weeks they had been going out, her fascination with him had grown. When she was with him she felt a pleasure she was sure no one in the world could understand.

At last they reached Brad's car. He unlocked and opened her door, and as she moved past him, he planted a light kiss on her lips. She stopped, the car door between them, and answered his kiss with one that was longer and more passionate.

When Brad slipped behind the wheel, their lips met again in a lingering kiss.

As he started the car and put it in gear, Krystal leaned luxuriously back in her seat and watched him steer the car into the bumper-to-bumper traffic that stretched for miles from the stadium.

"What are you thinking about?" she asked him as she wrestled to take her arms out of her coat sleeves.

He glanced at her, then back to the traffic. After a moment's thought, he answered, "That I don't want to take you home yet."

She smiled. "Don't. Let's go somewhere."

He turned his head and he examined her features with flitting eyes, as if he were trying to read a message in her expression.

He pulled off the expressway and they drove through a rural area that was unfamiliar to Krystal.

"Do you know where you are?" she asked.

"Em, generally, yes, sort of."

They drove past fields of rolled hay and stubs of cornstalks. It seemed to Krystal that the two-lane road went on forever, with no other crossing it for miles and miles. She clasped Brad's right hand between both of hers and snuggled against his shoulder until the smooth progress of the car slowed suddenly, jumped forward again, and after a few sputters, rolled to a stop.

Krystal sat straight and released Brad's hand.

He moved the gearshift, turned the ignition off, pressed the accelerator, and tried to start the car. Krystal hoped for a moment, but soon realized it was not going to start. She looked at the control panel. The needle on the gas gauge pointed to E.

Brad's car had come to a stop in the grass lining a country road that was barely two lanes wide. The road was bounded on one side by a cornfield that seemed to stretch for miles and on the other side by a thick section of woods.

"I don't quite know how to tell you this," he began.

"I know," Krystal said. "We're out of gas." They looked seriously at each other until a tiny giggle escaped Krystal's lips. Brad smiled then, and they both broke into laughter.

"Okay," she said. "What do we do now?"

"Em, I suppose we have several options. I could start out walking and try to find a farmhouse to call for help. Or we could—" He turned and pulled a blanket from behind his seat. "We could wait until someone happens along and flag them down."

"How long do you think that will be?"

He opened his door. "We won't know until we find out, will we?" He pulled the blanket out after him and shut his door. She got out of the car, too, and sat beside him after he had spread the blanket in the grass.

The autumn Sunday afternoon glowed with a fading orange sun. The air hung still around them, as if Nature held her breath for the young couple.

Brad glanced up the road in both directions, then returned his full attention to Krystal. He smiled at her.

She returned his smile and lowered her back onto the blanket. He joined her quickly, leaning on one elbow. He plucked a daisy and began pulling off the petals one by one with a meaningful gaze at Krystal.

She laughed at Brad, and then closed her eyes lazily. *This is so nice,* she thought. *So romantic. I don't care if a car ever comes along. We can just stay here and watch the stars come out.*

She opened her eyes, glanced at Brad, then closed them again. She remembered her phone conversation with Jason. *I've never felt this way before. I've been out with a lot of guys—* a pain gripped her heart at the reminder of how many—*but none of them were ever like this. This is so . . . so different, so* right. *Poor Kathy . . . I feel so sorry for her. She and Bill have been dating for years, and she still isn't sure if he's the one.*

She tried, with her eyes still shut, to sense Brad's closeness, to smell his fragrance, to hear him breathing, to feel him next to her even where they weren't touching.

She jumped slightly when her thoughts were interrupted by the pressure of Brad's lips on hers. She responded, almost shuddering with the emotional response she felt toward him. Krystal felt as though the sun and its autumn warmth were melting her into the blanket and the ground beneath. *I want to be so close to him,* Krystal thought, not in her head, but in her heart. *I want to be a part of him, I want him to hold me so close that I forget we're two different people.*

They kissed again, and when they parted, Krystal was aware that Brad was looking up and down the roadway again.

"Is something coming?" she asked, fearing to know the answer. She propped herself up on an elbow.

"No," he said, and Krystal smiled at the answer she had wanted to hear.

Brad pulled something out of his pocket and held it between them. "Is it time for this?"

Krystal had been staring at Brad's face and had to refocus her gaze and her thoughts. She looked at the small, square package in Brad's hand. It was a condom.

Her eyes played ping-pong between the package and Brad's eyes, wanting to read a mistake somewhere, a misunderstanding on her part. But as her mind cleared, there was no mistaking his intentions. Finally, unable to look at Brad any longer and unable to form any words, her eyes blankly rested on the package in Brad's hand.

After what seemed an endless silence, Brad's face assumed a sympathetic expression. "I'm sorry," he said. "You seemed so . . . I had no idea this would be such a surprise to you."

Krystal pulled her eyes away from the package and looked unblinkingly at Brad again. She felt herself blush.

"I thought," he said slowly, "we were on the same wavelength. The time just seemed right to me." He pressed. "Does it to you?"

When she didn't answer, he continued. "Look, Krystal, we've been getting very close in recent days, and I think you feel for me some of the same things I feel for you. I'm in love with you, Krystal, or I would never be so honest with you. We're not children, and if this is something we both want, what's stopping us?"

He scooted his body on the blanket to close the last tiny distance between them. The small package disappeared as he closed his hand around it. He lifted her chin with a finger and his blue eyes looked deeply into hers.

"I want us to be close, Krystal. I love you." And he kissed her.

Krystal tried to recover from her shock at Brad's boldness in proposing sex even as she struggled to understand her own feelings. *If this is something we both want,*" he said, "*what's stopping us?*" *Maybe he's right. If he loves me and I love him, isn't that what counts? This isn't like all those other times. This is special; this is true love. We could be closer than ever before. That's what you want,* she told herself. *Isn't it?*

Krystal surprised them both as she interrupted their kiss by beginning to stand.

"I think we'd better start walking," she said. "It's going to be getting dark and cold soon and we need to get gas for the car."

"But Krystal . . ."

"Or maybe I'd better stay with the car in case somebody comes by."

● ● ● ● ●

Ratsbane stared at the monitor in disbelief. It pictured the stranded sports car and Brad walking away from Krystal—and they were both still fully clothed.

The ant-toad demon sat frozen to his seat, mindful of Mallus's hovering presence in the motorized chair somewhere above him. He feared to look in Mallus's direction, but he feared more what might sneak up on him from behind.

He swiveled his neck slowly and lifted his eyes furtively into the air. He followed the lines of the jointed mechanical arm extending from the base of the PIT console until he spied the seat, poised in the air before the topmost row of monitors. It was empty.

Ratsbane breathed a sigh of relief and turned again to the keyboard. "Where did I go wrong?" he muttered. "I thought it was going pretty well."

Suddenly a forceful blow from behind smashed Ratsbane's face into one of the computer screens.

Mallus, who had swooped down behind Ratsbane on silent

wings, yanked his subordinate's head out of the shattered glass and swung him around to face him.

"You pathetic fool," Mallus hissed, his wings fully extended. "You don't just have him whip out a condom and say, 'Is it time?' What are you using for brains? You take these things a step at a time, a bra hook here, a belt buckle there, a button, a layer at a time!"

Ratsbane's ant face was disfigured by cuts and fear, but a demonic anger also rose in him. He and Mallus were nose to nose. "I make no apologies," he shouted back with a trembling voice. A broken antenna dangled in front of his face. He called Mallus a string of obscene names. "You've left me in the dark the whole time I've been here. If you want a better job out of me, give me some training; fill me in on your two-pronged strategy."

"I've given you—" Mallus blustered.

"You've given me nothing," Ratsbane countered, snapping off his broken antenna and waving it in front of Mallus's face like a weapon. "I've been doing the standard scheme, by the book every step of the way. You want fancy steps, you better give dance lessons!"

Mallus spat venom at Ratsbane, and they stared hatefully at each other for a long, tense moment. At last Ratsbane noticed Mallus's long neck muscles relax slightly.

"Another Westcastle catastrophe," Ratsbane offered in a conciliatory tone, "would look bad for both of us."

Mallus folded his huge wings slowly and drew his reptile face away from Ratsbane's nose. He began to pace back and forth across the PIT platform on his spindly legs, flicking his snake tongue in and out as he thought. Finally he halted in front of Ratsbane and groaned deeply. "You foul, loathsome demon of hell."

"Thank you," Ratsbane replied in a pleased tone.

"All right, I'll try to make it simple for your ant-sized intelligence, but I'm only going through it once. This entire two-pronged strategy may be hard for you to grasp, so I'll explain it one prong at a time."

He resumed his pacing and began speaking in the manner of a professor lecturing to a classroom of students.

"For centuries our directive has been to keep the Power Source of the Enemy disconnected from humans by overloading their lust capacity. So I use sex on them, you ugly fiend, *sex!* I keep channeling their desire for sex in every direction except in the direction the Holy One has charted for them. That way I not only keep them from reconnecting to their Power Source, but in most cases I kill the very thing I love to hate."

"What do you love to hate?" Ratsbane asked.

"Love, you dim-witted demon!" Mallus shouted. "I love to hate love!" He continued his pacing.

"So the first part of my strategy is to convince humans that their lust is both right and respectable. So your job here is to first get them to believe 'love makes it right.' Got that? You've got to make them believe that love makes sex okay. You can't rely only on lust anymore; lust has been around since Day One . . . okay, well, since Day Six, anyway. You've got to get them to believe lustful expressions are right because of love.

"Do you see what this strategy does? It gives humans of all ages a seemingly moral motivation to do something immoral. That's why we call it 'The Big Mo.'

"You see, Ratsbane, our strategy is truly diabolical. By convincing these humans that love makes it right, we can get them to express sex outside of the Holy One's established boundaries that were created to make sex so meaningful for them. And the great ugliness of all this is that you can see true love and intimacy die right before your beady eyes—sometimes love is killed forever!" His raspy voice increased with every word.

"Here in Subsector 1122," Mallus continued, "you will learn to be like me—a love killer!"

Ratsbane stood still, in wonder and amazement, as Mallus finished. A demonic chill crept down his spine as the demon's wicked laughter echoed through the vast cavern.

* * * * *

Krystal watched the sun sink below the cornfield and felt the air chill as night approached. She'd surprised herself with her treatment of Brad. She certainly didn't act the way she'd been feeling. But she thought now that her reaction had been a hundred percent right.

She bundled herself in the blanket and sat in the car with the doors locked, wondering what would happen during the course of the night.

I don't even know where I am, she thought, easily blaming

Brad for every problem. *Maybe he ran out of gas on purpose. Maybe it was all part of his plan. A deserted country road, a car out of gas—he even had the blanket in the car!* A thought struck her. *Maybe we're not really out of gas!* She looked at the gas gauge. *It's on E, sure, but maybe I can get it started.* She started to scoot over into the driver's seat when she noticed that there were no keys in the ignition. *He took the keys with him! Of all the—he took the keys with him! Even if someone came along right now with a can of gas, I couldn't go anywhere because he has the keys!*

She rubbed a circle in the window that had become fogged by her breathing. She peered into the coming darkness. *What's taking him so long?* She shivered with fear. *I'm here all alone. What if someone does come along? I'd be at their mercy. I should probably just stay inside with the doors locked and hope they go away.*

She let her head droop against the window as she spoke out loud. "Mom Davis and Darcelle are going to be worried sick about me. They'll probably call out the National Guard." She closed her eyes.

What am I going to tell them? she thought. Her anger at Brad began to cool, replaced with disappointment. *I guess Jason was right all along. I was kidding myself to think that we had something special.* Her eyes and nose began to swell with emotion. *Brad's no different. He just talks with an accent, that's all.*

She dozed and fell asleep without wiping the tear from her face.

A grinding engine noise woke her. It took some time after

she opened her eyes and lifted her head to remember where she was and what had happened. It was dark outside. She rubbed the window and peered out. A faint haze decorated the eastern sky, but she could see nothing on her side of the car.

She scrambled across the driver's seat and cleared that window. A big farm tractor rumbled in the road. Brad stood by while a man in a ball cap tilted a huge gas can into the sports car's tank.

She crossed back to her seat and leaned back against the headrest. She rose again briefly to unlock Brad's door, then returned, curled up in the blanket, and leaned her head against the window. She heard Brad and the farmer exchange some muffled words, and the tractor gnashed and belched and drove away.

She pretended to be asleep when Brad climbed into the car. The engine jumped to life when he turned the key, and he drove her home without a word exchanged between them.

▶ THE INSIDE STORY ◀
Love Makes It Right

I want to ask two questions, and I want you to answer each one carefully before you continue reading.[1] Ready?

First, **Does love make it right?** When you're in a relationship and it comes time to make choices about sexual involvement, does love make it right? Do you believe that loving someone makes sexual involvement right?

Second, **What is love? How do you define it?** Don't just shrug this question off, it is important. We use the word all the time—"I love my dog," "I love chocolate," "I loved that movie," "I love you, Esmerelda"—but what does it mean? Take a moment before you read farther to form a definition of what it means to tell another person, "I love you."

Now, I may shock you with *my* answer to the first question: I believe that love *does* makes it right. But you cannot understand my answer to that question unless you grasp my answer to the second question.

Many couples have come to me after they've become sexually involved and explained their actions by saying, "Oh, we just love each other so much we got swept away." I respond, "No, it's not because you love each other too much; it's because you love each other too little."

Many people subscribe to the idea that in every moral situation, if you do the loving thing, you do the right thing. There's just one problem: They often don't define what the loving thing is that makes sex right.

The Bible, on the other hand, not only affirms that love makes it right, it goes on to define what *is* the loving thing. "Pay all your debts, except the debt of love for others. You can never finish paying that! If you love your neighbor, you will fulfill all the requirements of God's law" (Romans 13:8). In other words, love *does* make it right. But the same passage of Scripture goes on to define love: "For the commandments against adultery and murder and stealing and coveting—and any other commandment—are all summed up in this one commandment: 'Love your neighbor as yourself.' Love does no wrong to anyone, so love satisfies all of God's requirements" (Romans 13:9-10).

You see, the Bible tells us that love makes it right, but it also defines what love is. And that's a crucial point. The word *love* is like a line drawing in a coloring book; it has no content. The law gives content to love; the commandments color in the picture.

What else does the Bible say about love? In 1 Corinthians, the apostle Paul gives a good description of what love does and does not do. "Love is patient and kind. Love is not jealous or boastful or proud or rude. Love does not demand its own way. Love is not irritable, and it keeps no record of when it has been wronged. It is never glad about injustice but rejoices whenever the truth wins out" (1 Corinthians 13:4-7).

Paul also wrote that "love does no harm to anyone" (Romans 10:13). Instead, we are to treat all people as we would like to be treated. Remember the Golden Rule? "Do for others," Jesus commanded, "what you would like them to do for you" (Matthew 7:12). Again, Paul put it this way: "Don't think only about your own affairs, but be interested in others, too, and what they are doing" (Philippians 2:4).

With these verses and others as a guide, we can develop a concise definition of love. Love is when the happiness, security, spiritual growth, and physical health of another person are as important to you as your own. The Bible commands, "love your neighbor *as* yourself"; it doesn't say to love your neighbor *more* than yourself. We are to love God more than we love ourselves, but we are to love our neighbor, boyfriend, girlfriend, or spouse *as* we love ourselves.

Ephesians 5:28 helps us understand the nature of love even better: "In the same way, husbands ought to love their wives as they love their own bodies. For a man is actually loving himself when he loves his wife." What does it mean to love your own body as the Scripture commands us to do? The next verse explains: "For no one ever hated his own flesh, but *nourishes* and *cherishes* it, just as Christ also does the church" (Ephesians 5:29, NASB, emphasis added).

To nourish your own body means to bring it to maturity, to bring it to mature happiness, security, spiritual development, and physical health.

That's what the Bible says Jesus did: "So Jesus grew both in height and in wisdom, and he was loved by God and by all who knew him."

The word *cherish* is used in popular love songs, of course, and it might conjure a picture of a little ponytailed girl squeezing a teddy bear. That's not what it means to cherish. It's not something sloppy and mushy at all; to cherish your body literally means to protect it from the negative and destructive elements. The picture is of a mother bird swooping down on her nest and spreading her wings over her chicks to protect them from the approaching storm.

If we truly love ourselves in the way God intended, we will nurture ourselves to mature physically, spiritually, emotionally, socially, and intellectually. We will also protect ourselves from anything that would hinder that maturing process.

When my daughter Katie was six years old, she heard me deliver a message on Matthew 22:37–39 about loving your neighbor as you love yourself. On the way to the car afterward she wore a puzzled look. I said, "What's wrong, honey?" She answered, "Daddy, if you don't love yourself, then your neighbor really has a problem."

She was absolutely right because loving yourself becomes the basis for loving someone else. Ladies, if you go out with a guy who really doesn't love himself in a genuine, biblical way, you'd better be careful. I wouldn't want that guy to be alone in the same room with my daughter. Gentlemen, if you spend time with a young woman who doesn't love herself, you'd better watch out.

On the other hand, can you imagine spending time with someone who loves you as he loves his own body? Imagine that the guy (or girl) you're dating is concerned about your spiritual growth, your maturing, your being nurtured. He's careful about where you go on a date, what you do, your conversation, and the way he dresses, because he nurtures and cherishes you and wants to make sure nothing hinders your happiness, security, spiritual growth, and physical health. Girls, could you trust a guy like that? You bet. Guys, could you trust a girl like that? Of course. Wouldn't you love to be married to someone like that? I thought so.

You see, if a person tries to push you into rejecting God's standards for sexual behavior, he or she is not loving you. No matter what that person may say, he doesn't love you too much, he loves you too little. And often, because we love ourselves too little, we let others push our standards outside of God's boundaries. That's why I have tried to bring up my children to love themselves. Until they do, they're not ready to date because they're not ready to love someone else.

Let me illustrate. God gave commandments such as "Run away from sexual sin!" because He wanted to protect and provide for us, to nurture and cherish us. The Bible says, "Run away from sexual sin! No other sin so clearly affects the body as this one does. For sexual immorality is a sin against your own body" (1 Corinthians 6:18).

A few years ago there were only five sexually transmitted diseases. Then, that number increased to thirty-eight. Now there are more than fifty diseases that people are passing around through sexual contact. And you've probably already heard it, but it's true nonetheless: When you have sex with a person, you're having sex with every partner that person has been involved with for the last fifteen years. That is one reason why, if you truly love yourself, you wouldn't dream of getting sexually involved with someone outside the God-given boundaries of marriage. And if you truly love another person, you wouldn't dream of encouraging him or her to begin or continue sexual immorality. That would not be nurturing and cherishing that person; it would not be protecting and caring for him or her.

Love makes it right. Absolutely. Love is the fulfillment of the law. Love does no harm to a neighbor. Love sees the sexual boundaries God gave and honors them. Therefore, love makes it right to wait until, on your wedding night, you can be completely confident of a monogamous (married to only one person) man and a monogamous woman in a mutually loving, monogamous relationship. What a loving and special gift to offer your husband or wife!

Love makes it right to wait until commitment confirms and faithfulness seals the love in a relationship.

WASHED UP
AND WASHED OUT

'm sorry, Krystal." Jason Withers was a clown, but he knew
when clowning wouldn't help.

"What are you sorry for? You were right," Krystal told him
with a sniffle for punctuation.

"I'm sorry because you deserve better than that."

"No, I don't," she answered. They stood beside Krystal's
locker in the school hallway. Bright yellow lockers spanned the
length of the hallway on both sides; red lockers began where
the hallway turned toward the school office. School was out,

and the hall was practically deserted. She looked up and down the hall, then bowed her head and confessed, "The worst of it is, if he'd done it a different way, you know?—not been so bold?—I don't know if I should be telling you this, but I think if he'd taken it slower, I would have probably said yes."

"You don't know that, Krystal."

"Okay," she answered in a sarcastic tone. She rolled her eyes. "How can I explain this to you?" They stared at each other until her eyes welled up with tears. "Until last night, Jason, I thought this was it. I thought I'd found a love I gave up finding a long time ago."

"Yeah, I know. That's why I said I'm sorry."

The two friends faced each other silently. Krystal's lower lip began to quiver, and Jason put his arms around her and held her in the hall.

They stood a long time in that posture, until Jason relaxed his embrace and cleared his throat meaningfully. Krystal leaned back and looked at him. He signaled up the hall with his eyes and a nod of his head.

Krystal turned and saw Brad Stuart strutting toward them, hands in his pockets, looking like a page in a men's fashion magazine.

"You want me to stick around?" Jason whispered in her ear.

"No," she replied firmly. Then, softer, "Thanks, Jason. I'll see you later, okay?"

Brad stood beside them. Jason touched Krystal lightly on her shoulder and departed. Krystal breathed deeply and turned her attention to Brad.

"Can we talk?" he asked.

Her lips drew a thin line across her face and she nodded.

"I am so sorry," he said, enunciating every word, "for last night. Is there *any*thing I can do or say. . . ?"

Krystal turned her face away and her shoulders began to shake. He stepped toward her and opened his arms to embrace her, but she stiffened and backed off.

"Em, this isn't the place," he said. "Can we go somewhere?"

"No," she said.

"Krystal," he pleaded, "I feel awful."

She offered no response.

"I had no intention of hurting you or offending you. I merely thought that our relationship was ready, that you felt the way I did. Was I wrong?"

He waited for an answer. Finally, as he was about to try again, Krystal spoke.

"It's just not that simple, Brad." She felt her anger fading and tried to hold on to it. She was not done being angry.

"Why not? I love you. What else do you need?"

Krystal shifted her feet impatiently.

"Okay," she said, "for one, I'm a Christian."

"Right," he said, as if he expected more to be said. "So?"

She rolled her eyes. "You can't expect me to just hop in bed with you. It's not right."

"Why not?" he pressed.

"Because we're not married."

"Oh please, Krystal, will you listen to yourself? You're talking like a child. I thought love was what Christianity was all about. Well, we love each other. That's what makes it right, not some piece of paper from the magistrate."

Krystal felt her arguments and answers crumbling beneath her, but that feeling revived her anger. Brad grasped her shoulders in his hands and pushed his face within inches of hers.

"If you didn't want it," he said forcefully, "if you didn't want to be with me as badly as I want to be with you, I'd leave you alone and never bring it up again. All you have to do is look me in the eye and tell me you don't want to. Go ahead. Do it."

He gazed into her eyes, and her glance flitted to and from his intense focus.

"See? You can't do it. Why do you fight something that we both want?"

"That's not all there is to it." She threw up both her arms to break his hold on her shoulders. "Okay?" Anger rose within her and seemed to release pleasure with every angry word she uttered. "I had a friend die of AIDS," she announced through gritted teeth. "I'm never taking that chance—ever—again."

"I use protection," he said in a wounded tone. "I always use protection. I had it with me last night, *remember?*"

"That's not good enough. So did he." The last three words came out in a low growl. She closed her eyes to contain her rage.

"So what are you saying? You want me to get tested?"

Krystal didn't know where this argument was going, but she knew she didn't want to go with it. She turned her back to Brad and stormed away.

He ran after her and turned her around by her elbow.

"Will that make you feel better?" he persisted. "If I get tested? All right, I'll get tested! Will that make you happy?"

He stretched his last word toward her as if he were expecting to hear an echo. Krystal turned the corner of the hallway just as the last syllable escaped Brad's mouth.

"Krystal! Stop right there!" Will McConnell shouted at Krystal from the top of the steps to the basement of Foster Hall, the old church building that was now part of Westcastle Community Church.

Krystal suspended her bare foot over the water that filled the basement. Liz Cunningham had called the youth group after school to come and help bail out the flooded church basement. Krystal and Darcelle had been the first to arrive; Darcelle, still in the process of removing her shoes and socks, sat on the landing behind Krystal.

"Don't move!" Will warned. He vaulted down the steps and landed beside Krystal. "Has anyone gone into the water yet?"

"No," Krystal answered, bewilderment showing on her face. "I was just about to."

"Well don't," he ordered. "I need something metal." He looked questioningly at Krystal, Darcelle, and Amber, who had come in with Will and descended the steps after him. No one answered him. "Coins. Anybody have some change?" He thrust his hands into his pockets. "No, never mind; I've got it." He pulled out a small ring of keys and tossed it into the water at Krystal's feet.

He shrugged. "Okay, now I guess you can go in." He sat down on the steps to take his socks and shoes off. Krystal still looked at him curiously.

"That was to make sure," he explained, "there was no danger of electrical shock."

Oh great, Krystal thought. She hadn't wanted to come with Darcelle in the first place. *I don't feel like being around people right now,* she had told Darcelle. *Especially not the kids from church.* Darcelle had finally convinced her, though. She hadn't counted on almost getting electrocuted.

Darcelle looked at the flooded basement, then back at Will. "Don't be silly, Will," Darcelle said. "That doesn't do anything. Besides, Liz said that the pastor has already been down here and had it checked."

Will smiled, shrugged, and waded in, stooping to retrieve his keys. The water nearly reached his rolled-up jeans. He stopped and rolled them farther, above his knees.

"Come on in, the water's fine!" He waved to the girls, who waded in after him.

"It's cold!" Krystal said.

"I can't believe how deep it is," Amber added.

"The first thing we need to do is figure out where the water's coming in."

"Shouldn't we try to get everything up out of the water?" Darcelle asked.

"Oh. Yeah. Why don't you and Krystal do that; Amber and I will look around."

Krystal and Darcelle started on the task of stacking chairs

onto tables, picking things up off the floor, trying to move everything to "higher ground." When Will and Amber had gone around the corner, Darcelle spoke in a quiet voice.

"You didn't finish telling me about your conversation with Brad."

Krystal grabbed a molded plastic chair with both hands and lifted it to fling it onto the table. She had opened her mouth to answer Darcelle when a look of surprise opened her eyes wide, and her feet slid out from under her.

She let go of the chair as she was falling and landed on her back. The chair dropped on her a moment after she splashed under the water.

Darcelle sprang to help her, but lost her footing on the slick floor and slid into Krystal's side like a runner stealing second base. They both struggled to their knees and helped each other, sopping wet, regain their footing.

"Looks like fun! I'm coming in!" Jason Withers flopped down the steps and splashed into the water wearing swim fins and goggles. In his hand he squeezed a chirping rubber tub toy, a bird of some kind, as he approached them.

The two girls shivered in each other's arms. Krystal had felt like crying with the combined frustration of the day as she and Darcelle had stood out of the water; the sight of Jason and his ridiculous outfit prompted a smile. She swatted playfully at his big smile.

"You two look like a couple of wet rats," he said.

"Are you here to go swimming or work?" she demanded.

"I was hoping to do a little of both," he said, punctuating his response with a squeak from the tub toy.

"Here then," she said, lifting a chair and shoving it into his hands. "Get started with the work part."

They worked, stacking chairs, toys, books, fabric, and boxes onto every available surface. Liz Cunningham and Joy Akiyama joined them shortly after Jason arrived, and the group worked steadily, exchanging only occasional words of instruction or information.

"I've got some good news and some bad news," Will announced when he returned to the area where the girls were working. "We found where the water is coming in. The bad news is, I don't think there's anything we can do about it. It's coming in through the wall and the floor."

The group followed him to a corner of the building where the surface of the water rippled with movement. Will pointed to the seams in the wall and floor. "See?" he said. "I don't know if there's a pipe broken or what."

"I think all we can do right now," Amber offered, "is try to move as much stuff out of the basement as we can."

Suddenly Krystal looked at Will and Amber, standing together with their pants rolled up, and an ache surfaced in her chest. *They look so happy together,* she thought. *They have something really special.* She recalled her morning scene with Brad and wished she could go alone somewhere to cry.

Duane Cunningham and Reggie Spencer came straight to the church after work ended on their construction site, and joined the effort. Duane made a few calls, and soon a large truck came and uncoiled a long hose into the basement and began sucking the water out and into the manhole down the street. They didn't finish until sometime after 8:00. Since none of them had eaten, they all went down to Pizza Palace together for a late dinner.

"You didn't talk much tonight," Darcelle said on the drive home. "Are you all right?"

Krystal shrugged. "I don't know. Maybe I'm just tired."

"Yeah, you sure didn't get any sleep last night. Think you'll feel better in the morning?"

"I don't know," she answered in a flat voice. "I just want to go to bed." She leaned her head against the car window and they drove the rest of the way home in silence.

●　●　●　●　●

Ratsbane was aware of a dark shadow overhead. He quickened his pace on the keyboard in an attempt to look impressive just as Mallus dropped onto the PIT platform with a flurry of feathers. He turned to Ratsbane with a hiss. "Are you making any progress?"

The toad with the ant head gulped loudly and filled Mallus in on several cases that he was overseeing personally, referring finally to Krystal's case number. "8463 is proceeding very nicely. Soon I'll have her convinced that love makes it right, and then she'll do it with that Brit. We could have suffered some damage tonight—she was at the church with some of those Westcastle kids. You know the ones I mean. But

I managed to keep her in line, kept her from confiding in anybody. I don't think it hurt us at all."

"What about those other two? Have you been working on them?"

"Oh yes, and it's a good thing I've been able to use the Big Mo on them because both of them have been stubbornly trying to stand up to all demonic suggestion and stop their sinning. But I think I have them convinced that they're not children anymore. 'If you love each other,' I've been telling them, 'and you both want it, there's nothing wrong with it.' I think they're starting to believe it."

"Excellent," Mallus hissed. "That's exactly the opening we want. Once we get them to believe this lie, we can go on to the next and the next, until their understanding is so clouded that they couldn't recognize the truth if it yanked them by the hair and screamed in their face.

"We just inject a little compromise here, a little immorality there, and we can destroy all the effectiveness of that stinking Liberation Commando group until they're just a handful of tepid church kids and their friends are all fodder for the fires of hell."

Ratsbane, excited by Mallus's oratory, performed a brief demon dance, folding and unfolding his legs in frog-like leaps punctuated by ecstatic squeaks, croaks, and curses.

"Stop that, you miserable wretch!" Mallus demanded. "Do you want someone to report you for being happy? I want to see what those insufferable humans are doing. Bring them up on the screen."

Mallus waited, turning his snake head from side to side, viewing Ratsbane's work first with one eye, then with the other. Ratsbane pounded the keyboard with wart-covered fingers and finally stood back as the images on the screen crystallized.

•　•　•　•　•

"It's over, Krystal." Krystal couldn't place the voice on the other end of the phone. Mom Davis had called her to the phone, interrupting a deep conversation she'd been having with Amber, who was spending the night with her and Darcelle.

"Who's speaking?" she asked.

"Kathy."

"Kathy?" Krystal felt like she was trying to summon her brain from some distant place. She knew she should recognize the voice. Suddenly, the fog cleared. *Kathy. My sister Kathy.* "I'm sorry, Kathy. I didn't recognize you."

"I told Bill," the other voice said flatly. "I broke the engagement."

"You broke it off? Why?"

A long silence followed Krystal's question.

"Kathy?"

"Yeah, I'm still here. Listen, I'm sorry for bothering you. I'll, uh—I'll talk to you later, okay?"

"No, Kathy, it's all right . . . Kathy?" Krystal pulled the receiver slowly away from her ear and returned it softly to its cradle. She stood in the hallway a long time, trying to deter-mine—and understand—what she was feeling.

Krystal returned to Darcelle's room to rejoin her and Amber. She plopped cross-legged onto the floor beside them.

"What did I miss?" she asked.

Amber cracked a half-smile and glanced at Darcelle, who smiled back and nodded.

"I was just telling Darcelle," Amber said, "that Will and I—" Tears filled Amber's eyes, but she quickly regained control. "Will and I met with Duane and Liz after everybody left Pizza Palace." Another pause. "This is so hard, guys," she said.

Amber's two friends simultaneously reached out a hand toward her; Darcelle squeezed Amber's hand and Krystal touched her shoulder tentatively.

"We told them," she continued, referring to Duane and Liz, "that we needed someone to be accountable to, someone to check up on us every once in a while. We were kind of scared of where we were going."

Amber released Darcelle's hand, turned around, and reached for a tissue from the bedside table. "This is so embar-rassing," she said, then paused again. "Will and I have messed around a little bit," she said quickly, as if impatient to get the words out. "We haven't had sex or anything, but we have done some things we know are wrong. And we both feel awful about it." She lifted the tissue to her nose and tears began to stream down her cheeks. "I can't believe I'm actually telling you this," she said.

Me either, Krystal thought.

Amber continued. "I know now that we should have set boundaries, you know?" She sniffed again and wiped her nose. "Liz pointed out that we didn't establish our standards up front when we started dating. That was our mistake . . . *one* of our mistakes," she said with emphasis.

"And now lately," she went on, "we've both been feeling so guilty. It's like we can't even have a normal date anymore. Or even be ourselves when we're together." She took a deep breath and released it, displacing a few strands of hair that sloped over her forehead.

Darcelle took over for Amber, filling Krystal in on the rest of what she had missed while on the phone with her sister. "Duane and Liz told Will and Amber they ought to confide in their closest friends, who could make a pledge not only to keep it confidential, but to pray for them and kind of check up on them. You know, ask them every once in a while if they're keeping themselves pure. That kind of thing."

Krystal looked from Darcelle to Amber, who was nodding. For the first time since she had begun to confide in her friends, Amber's eyes met Krystal's.

"I thought we could do that for her," Darcelle went on. She picked up Amber's hand and reached out for Krystal. "We can start praying right now."

Krystal grasped her friends' hands.

"You want to pray, Krystal?" Darcelle asked.

"No," she answered quickly. "You go ahead."

DATE
FOR DEBATE

S he was spooked. Krystal turned the corner and entered
Mr. Detweiler's office with a nervous glance over her shoulder.

Several times on the way from her locker, a squeaky,
scratchy voice seemed to whisper her name. She was certain
she heard it, but when she spun around to locate the source,
she saw nothing except a few students walking the hall, drink-
ing from the water fountain, or spinning the combination on
their lockers.

She stopped now and dropped her books on Mr. Detweiler's desk. She struggled to corral her stampeding emotions.

I'll take one more look down the hall, she decided. She drew a deep breath and stepped to the doorway—where she met a rushing Jason Withers. He bumped into her and she landed back inside the office, sprawled on the floor.

"Krystal! I'm sorry," Jason said as he helped her back to her feet.

Krystal was shaking as she stood; she leaned heavily on Jason, draping her arms around his neck.

"Are you all right?" he asked, wrapping his arms around her to support her.

She nodded. "I'm okay. Really. I'm not hurt, but . . ."

She was interrupted by the sound of a surprised Brad Stuart clearing his throat. He entered through the doorway behind Jason and paused a moment to stare significantly at the two friends in each other's arms. He skirted them at last and proceeded into the classroom beyond them.

Jason smiled sheepishly at Krystal.

She broke their embrace and stepped back slightly. "I'm okay. I was just a little spooked . . ."

"Hey! We're starting." Chase Everett, Mr. Detweiler's star debate pupil, leaned in from the classroom with a hand on the doorknob. He obviously meant for them to stop everything and answer his summons.

Krystal and Jason exchanged glances and joined the others in the next room.

They sat in their usual adjacent chairs near the front; Brad stretched his legs in the aisle in the last row.

"It's time, people," Mr. Detweiler announced, "to be determining what event or events you'll be participating in. It's also time to be getting a general idea of what your topics will be."

Krystal shot Jason a glance that said, *I haven't got a clue what I'm going to do.* Jason had already decided that one of his events would be H.I. — "humorous interpretation," in which he would present a humorous ten-minute cutting from a literary work. Krystal wasn't a bit surprised at his choice, but she'd had trouble making her own selection.

"Can I say what I want to do?" asked Leeann. Mr. Detweiler nodded. The enthusiastic blonde gushed, "I want to do a Prose and Poetry on Jim Morrison." Mr. Detweiler's face wore a blank expression. "Of the Doors? You know, 'Light My Fire,' 'Love Me Two Times'?"

The teacher nodded for her to continue without giving any indication that he understood what she was talking about.

"Anyway," she went on, a hint of impatience in her voice, "I want to use parts of his biography, *No One Gets Out of Here Alive,* and some other prose *about* Jim Morrison and intertwine some of his own poetry with it. I think it'll be *so* cool."

Mr. Detweiler cleared his throat. "No doubt it will be cool," he said, echoing her emphasis. "But let me ask you, are you going to attempt to make the point that this Morrison guy is a great poet? Or that he's better than Frost or Whitman? Or that he symbolizes the decline of English poetry in this century? Or something entirely different?"

"How about arguing," Jason offered, "that he was a jerk?"

Leeann's face registered shock at Jason's suggestion.

"Or not," he added apologetically, realizing he'd not said the most sensitive thing. "I was just joking."

"Your job now, Miss Fowler," Mr. Detweiler interjected, addressing Leeann, "is to decide what your approach will be." He glanced sharply at Jason. "It is not enough to talk interestingly on a subject; you must speak convincingly as well. So you must ask yourself, 'What am I trying to convince my listeners of?'"

Leeann smiled cooperatively at Mr. Detweiler before lowering her gaze to her notebook. She began writing furiously.

"Anyone else?" A movement in the back of the room captured the teacher's attention. "Mister Stuart."

"I'm considering several events," Brad said in his precise accent. Krystal never turned around; she sat stiffly in her seat. "Original Oratory is one I'm certain I'll try. I plan to speak on whether sexual inhibitions are based upon reason or superstition."

Jason shot Krystal a glance. Her ears and cheeks reddened, but she stared at the blank chalkboard in the front of the room.

"That's a rather broad focus, isn't it?" Chase countered. "Should you narrow it to, ah, maybe Western culture?"

"Actually," Brad answered, "now that you mention it, I think that's too broad as well." Chase nodded as if Brad were a fish that had just taken the bait. "In the UK, for example—and we certainly qualify as Western culture—people are much more mature in such matters."

"Do you mean mature or immoral?" Jason shot at Brad.

"Thank you." Brad smiled sweetly at Jason. "You illustrate my point perfectly. Americans' sexual behavior and belief is restricted so severely by outdated ideas and fears that I question whether a truly healthy sex life can be enjoyed by anyone in this society."

"You're coming close to composing a proposition, Mr. Stuart," Mr. Detweiler said.

"Yeah, he's good at propositions," Jason snorted under his breath so only Krystal could hear.

"I think it's dreadfully sad," Brad continued, ignoring the teacher's attempt to move the discussion, "that people can love each other deeply and yet be so controlled by irrational fears and imagined morals that they would deprive themselves of a fulfilling and satisfying commitment."

Krystal rose slowly from her seat as Brad finished talking. She stood erect for a moment, then turned her eyes on Mr. Detweiler and said, "Excuse me." She strode out of the room without looking at Jason or any of the others.

Jason left the room a few minutes after Krystal. Brad had finished speaking and Chase was meticulously outlining his plans for this year's debate team.

Jason searched the halls for Krystal without success. He finally cracked the door of the girls' restroom and whispered, "Krystal?" He listened for a few moments, then repeated, "Krystal? It's me, Jason."

He began to close the door when a small voice came from inside.

"I'll be out in a minute," she said in a weepy voice.

Jason paced back and forth in front of the door until Krystal came out.

"Don't let him get to you, Krystal. He's a jerk."

"I can't believe he did that," she said.

"He's a jerk," Jason repeated, as if that would answer all questions.

"I can't go back in there, Jason. I couldn't face them right now."

"They're almost done anyway. We should just go home. Do you need to get anything out of your locker?"

She shook her head and they walked out together.

Kathy was waiting when Krystal arrived at the Davis home. She sat on the edge of Krystal's bed, fidgeting with a tissue in her hand.

"I hope you don't mind me waiting for you here," Kathy said. "I expected you to be home earlier."

"No," Krystal said, almost welcoming the distraction from thoughts of her disastrous afternoon. "No, I don't mind. I usually do get home earlier, but I had debate team after school."

"I didn't know you were on the debate team." Kathy seemed impressed.

"I wasn't. Just started, really." *Just finished, too,* she thought. *Maybe.* She tossed her book bag into the corner and sat beside her sister on the bed.

They smiled weakly at each other and the conversation

lagged. Kathy seemed to be inspecting the curtains and furnishings of the room. Her eyes darted from window to chair to desk to door.

"Are you and Bill still—?" Krystal wasn't sure how to frame the question.

Kathy nodded. "He's pretty mad at me right now."

After another pause, Krystal asked, "What made you break it off?"

Kathy inhaled deeply, turned and swung one knee up onto the bed to face Krystal. "I just knew I couldn't marry him, Krystal. We don't know each other, really." Tears welled in her eyes and she reached for another tissue.

"You've been going together for two years!"

"Yeah," she said. She studied Krystal's face as if weighing whether she could be trusted. "Am I keeping you from anything?"

Krystal shook her head. They both, almost simultaneously, scooted farther back on the bed. Kathy nestled into the corner and leaned against the wall; Krystal crossed her legs and grabbed her toes.

"Nobody knows this, Krystal, but Bill and I—well, we've been kind of fooling around for a long time. We've been, uh, sexual with each other, you know?"

Krystal hoped her surprise didn't show on her face. Kathy had always been the "perfect" daughter; Krystal never dreamed that she might have been sexually active—especially not with Bill. They were such a "squeaky clean" couple.

"I guess that's bothered me for a long time. But I guess I

still thought I loved Bill. I mean, that's why I went ahead and did it, you know?"

Krystal realized that her sister was having a hard time looking at her. She would occasionally lift her gaze to Krystal's face, but it would never quite meet her eyes.

"Ever since Bill asked me to marry him—" She sniffed loudly and stopped to blow her nose. "Ever since Bill asked me to marry him, I've been thinking about us and our relationship and what it would be like. And I guess I've realized that we don't really know each other, Krystal. I mean, we do stuff together and we've been sexual, you know, but I don't think we've ever gotten to really know each other."

What's to know? Krystal couldn't help thinking. *This is Bill Fuller we're talking about.*

"We go out, and we do it, you know, but it's like we never really talk because all he wants to do is—you know. We never got the chance to be *really* intimate, Krystal. I used to think we were being intimate, but we were just having sex. And now, I don't know him and he sure doesn't know me."

Krystal watched her sister's face as they met each other's glance. Kathy's lips started to quiver, her nostrils flared, and her eyes reddened. A moment later, Kathy sobbed in Krystal's arms. Krystal held her older sister tightly and was startled when she discovered that she was crying too.

"Krystal, honey, the phone's for you," Mom Davis called up the stairs. Kathy had left over an hour ago and Krystal had dropped off to sleep.

She made her way from her room and picked up the receiver. "Hello?"

"Is this Krystal Wayne?"

"Yes, it is."

"Miss Wayne, I'm with Canter Polling Services. We're conducting a survey. I wonder if you'd mind answering a few questions."

"Well, I—"

"Do you subscribe to the view that all men are scum and should be drowned at birth?"

"What? Who is this?"

Something in the sniggering laugh on the other end tipped her to the caller's identity.

"Jason! Stop playing around."

"How did you know it was me?"

"How many idiots do you think I know?"

"Thanks a lot! I thought I'd just call and try to cheer you up a little bit."

"Well, thanks. But I don't feel much like cheering up."

"Still bummed?"

"I'll be okay."

"I wish you could just forget him, Krystal. Don't let him get to you. He's not worth it."

"It's just—I mean, Sunday night I was mad at him, sure, but I might have forgiven him. But he's hardly even giving me a chance. It's like he's determined to make me hate him."

"Is it working?"

"Sort of."

"Sort of?" Jason's voice rose a pitch. "I can't believe you, Krystal. What's the matter with you?"

"What's the matter with *me?*" she echoed, surprised by Jason's tone of voice.

"What does it take to convince you that Brad's a jerk?"

"Jason," she began, but he wasn't finished talking.

"He's not for you, Krystal. You need somebody who cares about you, somebody who has the same kind of values you do."

"Yeah, right. Where am I going to find somebody like that?"

Jason answered her question with silence. Angry silence, Krystal thought. "Listen, Jason. I really appreciate your calling, but I really can't talk much right now. Please don't be mad at me, but I really don't want to talk about this anymore."

They said their good-byes and Krystal returned to her room, where she wrapped her arms around a cushion and threw herself face down on her bed.

• • • • •

I wanna hold you, wanna squeeze you,
   Wanna love you, wanna please you,
   Wanna be your man forever,
   Let's get naked, girl, together.

Ratsbane grinned with pride at the song he had just made up. He let out a conceited little chuckle.

"That's pretty good," he said. "I should have been a horny toad!" He laughed again at his own wit.

He summoned Belchabub with a screech into the microphone of his headset. The central monitor of the huge PIT console's fifty-plus screens showed a weary Krystal Wayne at the dinner table with Darcelle and Mom Davis. Krystal rarely joined the conversation, and she ate little of the pork chops, applesauce, and green beans on her plate.

Belchabub vaulted the platform steps too quickly, lost his balance, and rolled across the floor, slamming himself into Ratsbane and hurling both of them into the PIT console with a loud crunch.

"You bonehead!" Ratsbane shouted. With a struggle he recovered himself and pointed to the keyboard. "I want you here, on this side of the keyboard. We're going to hit her hard and often."

"Hit who?" Belchabub asked, punctuating his question with a gurgling burp.

"Ugh!" Ratsbane protested. "You are foul and disgusting, do you know that?"

Belchabub said nothing, but smiled with obvious pleasure. They both began to turn to the keyboard again when Belchabub realized his question hadn't been answered. "Hit who?" he repeated.

"8463, you dimwit." He pointed to Krystal Wayne's image on the screen. "I want you to counter any interference from the Enemy. And make sure the SE level stays low." He responded to Belchabub's puzzled look, "That's 'Self Esteem' level, stupid. Got it?"

The underdevil nodded, and Ratsbane turned to the

screen. Krystal's offer to help with the dishes had been declined. She climbed the stairs and entered her room.

"Good!" Ratsbane exclaimed. He began furiously typing commands and combinations into the sophisticated computer. A steady string of figures and characters traveled across the bottom of the screen under Krystal's slow-moving image.

Ratsbane muttered into the microphone as he worked. "Poor Krystal. You've lost the perfect man—someone who really loves you—because you wouldn't commit to him physically, huh?"

He sneered at his assistant, who was working away beside him, eyes riveted to the screen.

"But Krystal, he wasn't asking you to do anything you didn't want to do, was he? He wasn't asking you to do anything you haven't done before. Lots of times, huh, Krystal? *Lots* of times.

"What good do you think it's going to do to turn him down like that? You can't be a virgin again, Krystal. You're already soiled. Damaged goods."

Belchabub shot out a long, narrow tongue, licked his thin snout, and pressed almost against the monitor screen, staring hypnotically. Ratsbane stomped hard on his foot. "You're not a spectator here, you contemptible mass of sheet metal!"

Belchabub bawled in Ratsbane's invisible ear and punched his assigned button a time or two.

"A girl like you," Ratsbane addressed Krystal again, "can't afford to be wholesome and pure. If you don't give Brad what he wants, he'll just find it somewhere else. And anyway, if you really loved him, you'd let him."

Ratsbane turned to Belchabub. "Check the SE meter," he instructed. "How's she doing?"

Belchabub ran a finger down a row of meters with needles pointing to black and red lines. "Low. And falling fast. It's working."

Ratsbane clapped his scaly hands together then rubbed them, as if warming them over a fire. He rolled his chair closer to the console. "Keep it up, you devil. It's working. We'll keep sending these impulses till we can launch her into dream mode."

He glared at Krystal's unhappy image on the screen. "Putty in my hands," he said.

•　•　•　•　•

"You didn't show up for debate yesterday," Jason said as he approached Krystal, who was standing with Amber and Hillary Putnam at her open locker. It was Thursday morning, two days after she walked out of Mr. Detweiler's classroom.

Krystal shrugged. "I didn't feel too hot. I went home right after school."

"Oh," he said, searching her eyes. "I was afraid you were going to quit."

She glanced at her friends and shrugged again. "I don't know. Maybe I will."

Jason's jaw fell. "You can't do that."

Amber touched Krystal on her sleeve. "We have to get going. See you at lunch, okay Krystal?" She and Hillary backed out of the conversation.

"Listen," he said as the girls left, "I'm sorry about the other night."

"I am, too, Jason. I just haven't been in the mood to talk much . . . to anyone."

The first morning bell rang. "We've got to get to class." He glanced up and down the hall at students rushing to their classes. "Will you at least come today? Meet me here after school and we'll walk in together."

"I don't think so, Jason. I don't think I can." She turned and slammed her locker door shut.

● ● ● ● ●

A steady rack-tacking rhythm rattled the pitted ceiling and stony walls of Subsector 1122 with skull-jarring vibrations. The animal heads of mutant demons periodically popped out from behind their computer work stations to glare at the source of the irritating noise.

Ratsbane, in the absence of Foreman Mallus, reclined in a rolling computer chair, his amphibian feet propped on the PIT console. His hands clutched two thin bones, the leg or arm bones of some creature. With these he pounded rapid beats on the edge of the Prime-Evil Impulse Transducer.

Why don't we do it,
Why don't we do it?
Let's be lovers
Under the covers

And do it, do it, do it, do it,
Till your Mama comes home.

Ratsbane sang as he drummed, opening and closing his mandibles in a gleeful grin.

The dozens of computer screens on the PIT console flickered with varying images. On one screen, a college-age boy opened a public restroom door, then closed and locked it behind him before extracting a glass vial and razor blade from his jacket. He sprinkled a fine white substance on the counter and bent to snort it.

Another screen bore the image of a young teenager in the back of a small church. She rested her head on the pew in front of her, which she grasped with both hands.

Ratsbane snatched his headset off the keyboard and held it to his head with one hand.

"Belchabub!" he screamed into the headset microphone. "Give some quick attention to 6124. She looks like she's about to do something stupid—like pray." He listened a moment, then replied. "See that she doesn't." He tossed the headset back on the keyboard and resumed his rapping.

A moment later, every screen except the central monitor switched to a new image, an image it would maintain for approximately one minute unless Ratsbane interrupted the cycle. In this way, the PIT could monitor over one thousand human subjects in the space of twenty minutes.

A brief tremor in the PIT cave halted Ratsbane's drumming. He froze, his hands suspended in the air, and listened.

Seconds later, after no further vibrations, he lifted a bone to resume his percussion performance, when a melon-sized chunk of rock splattered on the floor beside him. Another tremor followed, more severe than the first, and soon hunks of rocks cascaded from the ceiling like hailstones.

Sirens began sounding throughout Subsector 1122 and sparks occasionally leaped from computers here and there around the cave.

"Lord, have mercy!" he shouted, then, realizing what he'd said, clapped a hand over his mouth. He clamped the headset on and worked frantically at the console as rocks rained all around and debris whizzed past him on all sides.

"Fallout!" he screeched into the microphone. He cursed loudly as he spied Belchabub crouching under a computer desk on the floor of the PIT cavern. "I said, FALLOUT IN 1122!" he repeated, then ripped off the headpiece and dropped to his knees. He scooted under the desk part of the console, his lone remaining antenna protruding like a submarine periscope from his protected position.

"Belchabub!" he squealed over the pandemonium. "Get up here NOW!"

Belchabub's armadillo form darted back and forth across the cavern floor, dodging falling rocks and tipping furniture. Finally he waddled awkwardly to the platform and tried to squeeze under the console desk with Ratsbane.

Ratsbane nudged him out of their shared refuge. "Get to the keyboard," he squeaked. "Call up 6124 on the screen. You were supposed to stop her from praying, you worthless can of worm-waste."

"I did," Belchabub protested as he struggled to the keyboard. "I overwhelmed her with reminders of her sin and convinced her that the Enemy could never hear her prayers." He typed in a series of commands and peered at the screen. The girl—6124—had abandoned her attempt to pray and stood outside a store window, absently gnawing on a fingernail.

"I was right," Belchabub shouted above the reverberations of fallout in the cavern. "6124 isn't doing any praying."

"Well, someone is," Ratsbane shouted back. He cursed again and again, vehemently.

* * * * *

Krystal had been unable to pray for a long time; this time when she knelt beside her bed immediately after dinner she felt no different. She had no words to say and she knelt in stiff silence for what seemed like hours.

I'm not giving up this time, she vowed to herself. *I'll stay on my knees all night if I have to, but I've got to do something. I can't keep going on like this. I've been so confused these past couple weeks, and I know a lot of it has to do with my relationship with Brad.*

I guess I got so wrapped up in him that I got sidetracked and my priorities got messed up. Part of me wanted to forget about God and what's right or what's wrong, and I started doing that. I started to forget you, Lord, and ignore you. I didn't want to talk to you because I guess I was afraid that obeying you would mean losing Brad. But I lost sight of you . . .

Krystal didn't even notice that she had shifted from thinking to praying, but her thoughts carried her into prayer and she lost herself in fervent conversation with God.

Over an hour later, Krystal rose from her kneeling position and stood beside her bed, wiping her eyes with a white tissue. The imprint of her knees still showed in the carpet.

* * * * *

"Hey! Where are you going?" Amber called to Krystal in the school cafeteria. Krystal was steering away from her usual table with Amber, Hillary, and Joy.

Krystal balanced her tray on the edge of the table. "I can't eat with you guys today. I have to talk to Jason. Have you seen him?"

"Jason Withers?" Hillary asked, waving a french fry in front of her face.

"Never mind. I see him." Krystal grabbed her tray and strode off. "Jason, can we talk?" she blurted as she reached her destination.

Jason blinked at her then looked at his friends, who surrounded the table.

"I'm sorry if I'm interrupting," she offered, "but I really need your help with something."

"Uh, sure," he said. He glanced at his lunch tray. "You want to eat here or somewhere else?"

"Over there." She pitched her head in the direction of a nearly empty table.

"Are you okay?" Jason asked when they were seated across from each other.

"I'm great," she answered. "Me and God had a long talk last night." She smiled. "How much do you know about debate?"

He stopped chewing in midbite. He shrugged his shoulders and mumbled something that sounded like "I don't know." He held up a finger until he finished chewing. He swallowed hard and said, "I thought you quit."

"I changed my mind," she said airily. "A girl's allowed to change her mind. But I'm going to need a lot of help. I've got a lot of catching up to do."

"Well," he said, "I can tell you what I know, but it's not very much. It's mostly from Mr. Detweiler's handouts."

She made a face. "I haven't really studied those like I should."

"Well, there are different ways to debate, I guess. I don't know how clear I am on all this, but there's one kind of debate that has two-person teams. They take turns making little speeches for or against a certain idea, and then each has a chance to make a rebuttal.

"Then there's the main kind of debate—or the one that's used most, I guess—and that one lets team members ask questions of the other side. They call that the Cross-Examination Format, I think."

"How many people in that kind of debate?" Krystal interrupted.

"It's called four-person debate: two teams of two."

Krystal nodded.

"The last kind—that I know of anyway—is called Lincoln-Douglas, and it just has one person on each side of the issue."

"And they take turns making speeches and giving rebuttals?"

"Yeah," Jason said, finally becoming curious. "What's this all about, anyway?"

A sly smile stretched across her face. "You'll see," she said. Then, assuming a more serious expression, "But I'm going to need a lot of help."

Jason looked dumbly at Krystal for a few moments before he caught her meaning. "Oh, yeah, sure," he answered brightly. "You know my number."

She heard it again just as she turned into Mr. Detweiler's room: the hoarse voice whispering her name. She yanked her head around and surveyed the hall. She eased back into Mr. Detweiler's doorway, then poked her head out again quickly.

She glimpsed a head then, in the doorway of the next classroom. She ducked back out of sight and slid down onto her hands and knees. She peeked back into the hallway, her head nearly on the floor, just in time to see Jason Withers' head snake into the hall and heard him whisper, "Krystal," in an eerie voice.

She stood, then, and stepped out into the hall.

"Jason Withers," she said in a loud preacherly voice, "get

on your knees right this minute and ask God's forgiveness for your sick and perverted behavior!"

Jason jumped out in full view and dashed to Krystal. "You don't have to get crazy on me," he whispered. "What do you mean, sick and perverted?"

She smacked him lightly on the arm. "You scared me to death when you did that the other day."

"Did what?"

She rolled her eyes. "That. What you were doing just now."

"I didn't do anything the other day. When was this?"

"Stop, Jason. I caught you. You don't know when to quit, do you?" She smiled pityingly at Jason as she turned and entered the classroom.

"I don't know what you're talking about," he insisted in a wounded tone as he followed her.

Mr. Detweiler acknowledged Krystal's presence with an appreciative smile. She watched him glance from person to person, mentally counting heads, as he prepared to start.

Krystal's hand shot up.

A surprised look splashed onto Mr. Detweiler's face as he called on her.

"I don't know what all of you have been doing the past couple days," she said buoyantly, "but I'd like to respond to Brad Stuart's comments on Tuesday."

Now it was Brad's face that registered astonishment. Krystal rotated in her seat to face him.

"I think the idea you proposed for an Original Oratory is

good—so good, in fact, that I think it deserves more discussion than an O.O. would allow."

Brad's eyes narrowed into a skeptical expression.

"So I'd like to challenge you to a Lincoln-Douglas debate on the proposition that Eisenhower High School should distribute condoms to its students."

Brad bent his head sideways, but his eyes remained fastened on Krystal. "Come again?"

"I challenge you to a debate," she repeated. "A Lincoln-Douglas debate. That would be just you and me debating." She stole a glance at Mr. Detweiler, searching for any indication that she was saying the wrong things. "And I suggest that we debate before the school board."

"I believe you're serious!" Brad's voice shook with the realization.

"At the next meeting of the board." Krystal grinned, obviously enjoying the surprised expressions that surrounded her.

"I'm afraid I must interrupt." Mr. Detweiler crossed his arms in front of his chest.

Krystal closed her eyes as if making a birthday wish. *He's going to shoot me down*, she feared. *He's not going to let me do it.*

Mr. Detweiler cleared his throat authoritatively and faced Krystal. "Your proposition," he started. "It would be a good proposition for a standard debate, but Lincoln-Douglas debates use propositions of *value*." He turned toward the chalkboard and picked up a piece of chalk.

Krystal clenched her jaw and struggled to frame a reply. She felt her euphoria slipping.

"A proposition of value," Chase Everett, the debate king, interjected in a condescending tone, "expresses an *opinion*, a judgment about—whatever. Uh, in this case, condoms or the distribution of condoms."

"So," Krystal attempted, "if the proposition were that distributing condoms to high school students is dangerous and counterproductive?"

"Pick one," Mr. Detweiler said. Krystal twisted her face into a question mark. "It's better to keep your proposition focused; then your argument will be easier to focus and, thus, more persuasive."

"Okay," Krystal said. "Distributing condoms to high school students is dangerous."

Mr. Detweiler raised his eyebrows, wagged his head, and pursed his lips in an expression that said, *Not bad*.

"Do you accept?" Krystal pressed Brad.

His answer was a tight-lipped nod.

A low whistle trilled between Jason Withers's lips. A shroud of silence descended on the room for a few moments as everyone pondered the exchange between Brad and Krystal. Finally Mr. Detweiler dismissed everyone. The room emptied slowly; most of the team members departed solemnly, as if emerging from a prayer meeting—or an execution.

ARMING
FOR BATTLE

Krystal!" Jason Withers jumped up from the couch in Liz and Duane Cunningham's apartment and charged Krystal, who had just entered with Darcelle. He seized Krystal's elbow before she could get her coat off and steered her into the kitchen.

"Boy, have we got a lot of work to do!" he huffed.

"Oh, I know, Jason. That's why I said I was going to really need your help on this thing, remember?"

"No, no, no! That's not what I mean." He stepped closer; they were nearly nose to nose. "Brad's already got Chase Everett helping him."

Her eyes swelled like twin balloons. "Oh, no," she moaned. Her heart had sunk low enough to create a sick feeling in her belly. "Chase Everett. What are we going to do?"

"Pray?" Jason suggested halfheartedly.

"We're going to need it, that's for sure."

They joined the rest of the group. Duane Cunningham sat on the edge of the couch, his hands pressed together in a frozen clap. Reggie Spencer and Liz sat on either side of him; Will, Amber, and Joy had arrived during Jason and Krystal's kitchen powwow.

"You're just in time, Krystal," Duane said. "I've been telling everyone else how I've been praying for direction from the Lord for myself, but especially to know what direction he wants this group to be going.

"He's really brought us a long way, and I don't think he's finished teaching us how to lead our friends to Christ; but I've felt for some time now that he might be about to spring something new on us. I think I just found out what it is."

He cleared his throat and continued. "Before any of you arrived, Jason was sharing with Liz and me, in his usual enthusiastic way"— the group exchanged knowing glances—"some things that he and Krystal have gotten themselves into recently." Duane threw a wink at Krystal.

"So," he went on, "I'd like to ask Krystal to share with the whole group what's going on, and then perhaps we can spend some time in prayer and even come up with some practical ways the Liberation Commandos can be involved."

Krystal blushed a rich color of red, not only at the sudden attention focused on her, but at the realization that the whole story would include the night she and Brad ran out of gas, the night he brandished a condom at her.

She began, however, and related the story, starting with the first debate team meeting and ending with her brash challenge of Brad Stuart. "And now," she finished, "Jason tells me that Chase Everett's helping Brad prepare for our debate. Chase is like the Michael Jordan of debate. So . . ." her voice faded like snow melting into the sidewalk.

"It's a beautiful day in the neighborhood," Jason sang, "a neighborly day in this beauty. Would you be mine, could you be mine? . . ."

His attempt at humor was rewarded with a few feeble, nervous chuckles from the group, but an awkward silence quickly filled the spaces their fading laughter left in the room.

Duane cleared his throat. "Let's go to prayer about this, then. I believe that God has put Krystal in a position to influence a lot of people, and while she may not feel equal to it, if we link our prayers to God's power on her behalf, anything is possible. So let's pray, and after a few of us offer prayer, I'll ask Amber to conclude."

Darcelle slid from her seat and knelt in front of the couch; others bent forward and bowed their heads over clasped hands. A few full moments later, prayer began to fill the room.

"Humans be damned!" Ratsbane screeched as he viewed the scene in Liz and Duane Cunningham's living room on his central PIT monitor in the sulfur-smelling gloom of Subsector 1122.

He cursed with frustration and terror. He observed Will McConnell clench his folded fists so tightly that his reddening fingertips contrasted eerily with whitening knuckles. Darcelle Davis pressed her face into the couch cushions as if trying to block out all distractions to prayer. Krystal covered her face with her hands, bowed herself almost double, and began rocking ever so slightly. Ratsbane recognized those and other signs of intensity and concentration with such fury that he wished he could reach into the computer screen and wrench each soul in that room into the hell he himself inhabited.

"Belchabub!" Ratsbane howled in agony and rage. A dark form appeared behind him. "WE'RE GOING TO GET BACKDRAFT AND WE'RE GOING TO GET IT FAST. BACK OFF THE POWER. BRACE THE SUBSECTOR FOR FALLOUT. MOVE, YOU BRAINLESS—" He stole a quick glance over his shoulder and saw that the form belonged to the snake-headed Mallus.

Ratsbane whipped his head around to check the monitor and growled as he saw, swirling around the praying group in the small apartment, a blue-white mist, faint at first. He shouted commands into his headset, punched buttons and twirled dials, then slapped toggle switches up and down in a frenzy.

The blue-white mist in the Cunninghams' living room floated into two distinct vapors, which in turn congealed into two massive, muscular forms in blue and white uniforms.

"Aaah, I knew it!" Ratsbane groaned. "Brigadiers! Brace for the backdraft." He turned from the PIT console and shouted in a voice that carried into every craggy corner of the PIT cavern. "BACKDRAFT! BACKDRAFT! PREPARE FOR THE BIG ONE!"

He stood stoically watching the screen like a captain going down with his ship and saw the blue and white brigadiers perform one of their heavenly dances around the praying group of Westcastle youth while every demon around him dove for cover. He cursed the brigadiers and cursed the humans, who by their fervent, concentrated, specific praying, had summoned the angelic warriors.

Ratsbane gripped the console, preparing for the backdraft, the onslaught of power that he'd experienced every time the brigadiers had short-circuited his demonic efforts to influence and enslave his human charges. He stood motionless, waiting, fearing, cursing, wishing he could duck for shelter himself, but not daring to move while Mallus watched.

"ALL IMPULSES HAVE BEEN JAMMED BY THE BRIGADIERS, MIGHTY MALLUS," Ratsbane shouted over his shoulder as dust and soot began to swirl around him. A sudden spark from the PIT console startled Ratsbane, and he nearly dove for cover. "I'M NOT GETTING THROUGH TO

ANY OF THE HUMANS. IT'S THAT STUPID STYGIOS IN SUBSECTOR 477," he whined. "HE'S NOT GIVING US ANY HELP AT ALL!"

Suddenly a frightening explosion rocked the PIT cave, sending jagged shrapnel flying all around them. Ratsbane risked a quick glance behind him; Mallus stood straight, unmoved, on the platform behind him. Sparks and flame shot around the cavern like a laser light show. Cries of fear and pain from wounded maintenance runts and underdevils pierced the air.

A deafening clang resounded behind Ratsbane, causing him to jump in the air and momentarily attempt to climb the face of the PIT console. He managed to maintain control of himself, however, and whirled to see what had caused the racket. The robotic arm with the chair on the end, which Mallus had used to float up and down the mammoth height of the Prime-Evil Impulse Transducer, had snapped in two and crashed onto the snake-headed form of Mallus. The foreman's scrawny bird legs extended from beneath the crumpled arms of metal, resembling the scene in *Wizard of Oz* when the wicked witch meets her end beneath a fallen house.

Freed from the scrutiny of his superior, Ratsbane immediately ducked under the PIT console and covered his ant head with his warty hands. Cringing in the cramped shelter, he peered out into the PIT cave and saw the runts and underdevils emerging cautiously from their hiding places; the fallout had subsided.

Swiftly, he dashed out from beneath the overhang, propped his hands on his hips, and squealed into the cavern.

"Come out, you cowering demons of Subsector 1122! The fall-out is over. Stop this pitiful display of cowardice and return to your stations!"

Ratsbane wheeled to view the earthly scene that had started the trouble; the praying had stopped amid hugs and tears, and the blue-white forms faded from the PIT screen.

"It's over," he said, as if to assure himself. He turned once more to face the crushed form of Mallus, buried under the mechanical arm. "Ding-dong," he muttered. "The witch is dead."

Just then, however, an alarming thought hit him: "Mallus never explained to me the second prong of his strategy! What am I supposed to do now?"

* * * * *

Krystal trembled from the combined excitement, fear, and determination she felt after Amber had softly spoken a power-ful plea for God's guidance and blessing. She and several others embraced and basked tearfully in the warm glow of the moment.

"Now," Duane said as the group calmed and people returned to their seats, "is there something else we can be doing to help you?" He addressed himself to Jason and Krystal.

Krystal and Jason exchanged empty looks. She turned to Duane with uncertainty written on her face.

"We shouldn't stop praying," Darcelle suggested. "I think we should pledge to pray at least every day for this thing."

"Yeah," Will agreed. "When is it going to happen?"

Krystal shrugged. "I don't know yet. I have to find out when the next school board meeting is."

"We're probably going to need a lot of help researching," Jason offered. "I mean, we're both new to all this and Chase Everett's been doing it for years. We're going to need help finding information and reliable sources and quotes and statistics and all that kind of junk and who knows what else and I think I'm going to have a nervous breakdown."

Amber laughed. "We can help with you that," she said, grasping Will's hand and squeezing it.

"Yeah," Will said, as if waking from a dream, "I might be able to get some help on InfoComp—that's the, uh, interactive computer service I subscribe to," he explained in response to the others' puzzled looks. "Who knows? I may be able to get the whole computer club in on this. I know Marlon will help."

"Should we try to get the word out?" Reggie asked. "I mean, this whole issue is pretty important. It's something you don't ever hear about on TV or in school. It seems to me like more people need to hear about this kind of thing. Am I right?"

"I hadn't thought about that," Krystal said.

"I'm thinking maybe we should plaster posters all over the place, pass out fliers, things like that."

"You're right," Darcelle added. "This is something *The General* should cover," she said, referring to the school newspaper. "We could make this thing really big. I bet I could even get the city paper to cover it!" Her eyes sparkled with excitement. She smiled enthusiastically at Krystal.

Krystal's eyes broke Darcelle's gaze and she stared down at the brown and beige carpet. Darcelle noticed her friend's change of mood.

"What do *you* think, Krystal?" she asked.

"All that would be great," she answered, "if I win." She turned her class ring around and around on her finger. "But what if I lose?" She swallowed. "Like I said before, Jason and I don't *really* know what we're doing. All that publicity could backfire."

Leaden silence settled again over the group.

"Krystal's got a point," Duane said finally. "By blowing this thing up, we're putting her on the spot. And taking a big risk. It could blow up in our faces."

"Duane." His wife, Liz, laid a hand on his knee. "I think what you're saying is, we're afraid God isn't going to answer the prayers we just prayed a few minutes ago." Duane straightened his back and looked at Liz. "I think we need to just commit those fears to him and trust him to accomplish whatever he wants. Win or lose, we should just do our best and let him take care of the rest."

Duane nodded thoughtfully. "What do you think, Krystal? I know it's easy for us to say just trust God, because we're not the ones who are sticking our necks out. You are."

Krystal nodded. She knew Liz was right; but she still cringed when she heard Duane say, "We're not the ones who are sticking our necks out; you are."

"I'm scared to death," Krystal said. "And if I start thinking about maybe losing, it makes me not want to do this. But this is something I really feel strongly about." Her face flushed and a fiery intensity rose in her eyes. "I'm not backing down."

Mr. Detweiler closed his office door behind Krystal. He darted to the chair beside his desk and lifted the sloppy stack of papers and file folders off the chair and set it atop a leaning tower of materials supported by the file cabinet. Her eye was drawn to a row of plastic yellow boxes on the table against the opposite wall; each box bore a strip of masking tape labeled "Afghanistan-E. Europe," "England-Kuwait," to the last box, which was tagged "Rhodesia-Zimbabwe."

The teacher lowered himself into his creaky wooden desk chair and opened his mouth with a smacking sound. "I wanted to talk to you, Krystal," he began, "about this debate thing."

Krystal's heart sank. *Here it comes*, she thought. *Why did Jason have to open his mouth to everybody?* She studied Mr. Detweiler like a boxer measuring an adversary. *He's not going to let us do the debate.*

"The venue you proposed the other day . . . I'm afraid things don't work quite that way." Mr. Detweiler rhythmically tapped the eraser end of his pencil on his desk.

Krystal's mind was still back in Liz and Duane's apartment, wondering how she would break the news to the Liberation Commandos. "The venue . . ." she began, trying to repeat what he had said. "I'm sorry, what did you say?"

"You challenged Brad to debate before the school board. That's not really how it works."

Her mouth formed a silent *oh* in response.

"I'm afraid the school board wouldn't allow you to take over their meeting for a debate, no matter how important the subject matter might be."

She nodded idly.

"How shall I put this?" He stared at the ceiling. "Um, the school board is *re*active; I guess that's the way to put it. They're not in the business of conducting research or hearing debates. If a problem arises in the district, they address it; but they would not want to invite controversy with the kind of thing you proposed."

"But," she said tentatively, like a skater testing the ice, "wouldn't this kind of thing qualify as a problem they would want to respond to?"

"No. You see, you and Brad are all hot and bothered about it, but to this point it hasn't become a problem at Eisenhower."

"When would it become the kind of problem they would do something about?"

"Well, I suppose if the principal approached them about it or parents began complaining . . ."

She nodded her head—not in agreement, but in understanding—and watched her ring as she turned it around on her finger. "So, you're telling me the debate's off."

"Oh, no, no, no!" he said.

Krystal's head snapped up.

"I'm just saying you won't be able to do it before the school board. At least not in this district."

"But we can still do it?"

He nodded his head. "We can set it up as an after-school

event or something along those lines. It might stimulate a little interest in debate. That would be a very good thing from my perspective."

Krystal jumped to her feet. "That's great, Mr. Detweiler! When can we do it?"

He consulted a large white calendar on the wall beside his desk. "Oh, how about a week from today?"

Krystal let out a low groan. "That seems a little soon," she said.

He shrugged his shoulders. "Two weeks from today," he declared.

"I've got a lot of work to do before then," she said, hoping he'd delay the event a week or two more. Instead, he stood and opened his office door.

"You got that right," he said.

* * * * *

Ratsbane's glassy black eyes swept the PIT cavern from side to side. Several computer cables were still severed, a fine layer of sulfur dust covered every surface, many computer stations remained inoperative, and maintenance runts tracked in and out of the cave, clearing the rubble and cleaning up the mess. Much of the debris from the fallout had been removed, and most functions of the PIT console had been restored.

"Where is Belchabub?" Ratsbane wondered aloud. He searched the gigantic room and finally heard footsteps behind him. He turned as Belchabub hauled his armadillo body over the last step to the PIT platform, but Ratsbane was still slightly off-balance when Belchabub's feet slid out from under him and he rolled toward Ratsbane, upending him like a bowling ball picking up a spare.

Ratsbane scrambled to his feet and snatched Belchabub's ears with two knobby fists. "You smelly sack of entrails!" he screamed. "You'd better learn to stay on your feet or I'll feed you to Plugly over there."

At the mention of his name, a demon with a hyena head and sloth body looked up from his computer station and licked his jowls hungrily. His sharp canine teeth glistened in the gray-green light of his computer screen.

Belchabub winced.

"Where have you been?" Ratsbane demanded.

"You sent me to ask if Central had any data on debate teams."

"That was days ago, wasn't it?"

"Yes, Foreman Ratsbane," Belchabub answered, acknowledging Ratsbane's ascent to Mallus's former position. "But I have a little trouble with motor skills," he sniveled, "as you know."

Ratsbane pointed his bulbous black eyes at Belchabub. "Did you get the information?"

"Central said that they have anything you could possibly want."

"So did you bring it?"

"Bring it?" A sheepish expression spread across Belchabub's face. "I was supposed to bring it? You only said to ask. You didn't say to bring it."

Ratsbane whacked Belchabub's head with a fist and began screaming, his voice like the squeal of brakes on a runaway truck. "You idiot! These human teenagers are staging a debate, and I have to stop it or win it. I can't do either unless you stay on your feet long enough to get me that information and get it quick!"

* * * * *

"You're crazy, Jason." Krystal stood in the middle of Jason's bedroom. She had called to tell him the news about her meeting with Mr. Detweiler, and he had insisted that she come right over to his house. His bed had been shoved off into the corner and a long folding table occupied the center of the room. The wall was a patchwork of full-sized poster boards of various colors, labeled "Affirmative Constructive," "Negative C.E. of Affirmative," and so on, concluding with "Affirmative Rebuttal." A long banner of computer paper stretched over the poster boards, emblazoned with the words "Great Debate Headquarters." The table was already blanketed with reference books, file folders, pens, and notebook paper.

"You're stark raving mad," Krystal said.

Jason thanked her with an elaborate bow. "Will did the big sign for me," he said, pointing to the banner. "I've still got a lot left to do, but hey, we're already firing on all pistons. Tomorrow the Commandos are meeting at Duane and Liz's and we're going to make posters and fliers, plot strategy, assign areas of research . . ."

"You're really into this, aren't you?"

"Who, me?" He shrugged and pursed his lips in thought. "Nah, it won't be a big deal to me when you kick Brad's butt. What makes you think that would be important to me?"

She laughed and threw her arms around his neck. They twirled each other around the room in a joyful hug until they nearly toppled the research table in their exuberance.

"Hold on," Jason said breathlessly when he heard the phone ring. "I've got to get that."

While he was gone, Krystal poked through the materials Jason had already gathered: books with titles such as *Getting Started in Debate*, *Basic Debate*, *Strategic Debate*, copies of a magazine called *Rostrum*, stapled sheaves of papers in fading purple ink. She held a videotape about debate and speech in her hand when Jason returned to the room.

He saw the videotape when he returned. "I haven't had a chance to look at it yet," he said.

"Where'd the rest of this stuff come from?"

"Everywhere, just about—from Mr. Detweiler, the school library, the regular library, Duane—I haven't gone through it all, but some of it looks pretty good."

"What's this Affirmative Constructive and Negative C.E. of Affirmative about?" She pointed to the seven poster boards covering Jason's wall.

Jason stretched across the table and snatched a thick set of stapled papers. "This is your homework for tonight," he said. "You've got to know this. Those—" he pointed to the poster boards—"are the parts of a Lincoln-Douglas debate. The Affirmative Constructive is your first speech, where you try to lay out all the reasons why condoms being distributed in high schools is dangerous."

"*I* speak first?"

He nodded. "The way you worded your proposition, you're the affirmative side. You're the one arguing *for* the proposition."

"Oh," she said. "I just didn't know I was going to be first."

"You get to speak for—" he flipped through some papers on the desk—"six minutes. Then comes the negative cross-examination of the affirmative. Brad will get to challenge you and ask you questions. Then—that lasts three minutes—then he does a seven-minute constructive speech, and it goes on from there: affirmative cross-examination of negative, affirmative rebuttal, negative rebuttal, and affirmative rebuttal."

"I can't believe all of this. You've really been working. I haven't done *any*thing yet."

"Oh, you will, Krystal. You're the one who has to know all this stuff. You're the one who has to put most of this stuff up here," he said, tapping his head with a finger.

She flashed a worried smile. "Thanks for cheering me up. What was it you were going to tell me when you first came back in?"

"Huh? Oh, yeah. That was Buster on the phone."

"He wasn't at the meeting last night," Krystal remembered aloud.

"Yeah, but I guess Duane or somebody called to tell him

what was going on. Anyway, he saw Brad coming out of the Walnut Street Clinic this afternoon and went in after he left. He said he's got all kinds of pamphlets and information and junk like that that he's going to bring by this weekend, stuff that Brad and Chase are probably going to use in the debate. So we can be ready for them and blow them out of the water when they bring it up! Ba-BOOM!"

Krystal jumped, not so much from Jason's loud sound effects, but mostly from the explosive activity of the butterflies in her stomach.

Liz and Duane's apartment buzzed with excitement on Saturday. Jason and Will had papered the walls with computer-generated posters and fliers in fluorescent colors. Amber had separated the room into three distinct areas: Publicity occupied the couch and stuffed chair in the center of the room, the kitchen table and chairs had been dragged into the room and tagged Research, and three folding chairs by the windows, Amber explained to Krystal, were the Technical section.

"Technical?" Krystal asked.

"You, Jason, and Duane are going to work through a crash course on debate—all the rules and strategies and the ins and outs of debating. Leave the publicity and the research up to the rest of us, at least for now. All right?"

Krystal looked at Amber with a dazed—but pleased—look. For the first time since the day she first challenged Brad, she began to feel that she stood a chance.

Krystal stood beside the Research table and eavesdropped

on a conversation between Will and Marlon Trask. Marlon, Will's friend from the computer club at school, had become a Christian because of the Liberation Commandos, and now he had begun a similar group at his church. Krystal listened as they brainstormed research sources: reference books, newspapers, pamphlets, government documents, indexes, and so on. Buster sat silently at the same table, poring over what appeared to be the pamphlets he had obtained at the clinic.

She next wandered over to the couch and knelt beside Darcelle as she outlined plans she had.

"I'm going to have to interview you, too, Krystal," she said. "I'll want to get some quotes from you *and* from Brad. Joy, I'd like you to take charge of distributing posters, fliers, and things like that; Will and Marlon have come up with several good designs, and they're also going to be printing out some banners to string across the hallway at school as we get closer.

"I've already talked to Mr. Sanders about announcing the debate on the school radio station, and he's okay with that. So before we leave today, I want us to have announcements of various lengths—I think Mr. Sanders said ten seconds, twenty, thirty, and sixty seconds—that can be read on the radio."

Krystal forced herself to break away from Darcelle's instructions and joined Duane and Jason by the windows.

"Did you do your homework last night?" Jason asked.

"Yeah, but it's going to take me a long time to get it all straight up here." She tapped her head with a finger like Jason had done last night.

Duane stood and surveyed the room. "I think we're all

here," he said above the electric chattering in the room. "We're going to do our most important work first," he said. "Let's spend some time in prayer."

"Mom? Is Kathy there?" Krystal dialed her parents' number as soon as she and Darcelle arrived home from the meeting at Duane and Liz's. She'd found herself thinking of her sister during the prayer time and had been unable to shake Kathy from her mind through the rest of the meeting. *I'll just tell her I've been thinking about her, ask how things are going now that she and Bill are history, and that'll be it. Let her know I'm trying to have a normal relationship with my sister.*

"This must be Krystal, right?" said the voice on the other end of the line. "This is Harriet Robinson, from next door. I'll, uh, I'll see if your mother can come to the phone, okay? Just hold on?"

"No, wait a minute," Krystal began, but a clunk in her ear told her that the receiver had been set down on the phone table in the hall. *I don't need to talk to Mom,* she was about to say. *I was just going to ask her to get Kathy.* She switched the phone to the other ear. *Harriet Robinson?* she thought belatedly. *What's she doing over there?*

"Hello?"

"Mom?"

"No, this is Harriet Robinson again. I feel really awkward here, Krystal. I came over to help when I saw the ambulance."

"Ambulance? What ambulance?"

"I don't—" Indecision rose in Mrs. Robinson's voice. "I

don't know how much I should really tell you over the phone. I imagine your mother would probably rather tell you herself. If I had a daughter, I'd want to be the one to tell her, I know that, but your mom isn't here now. I'd rather ask her—"

"Mrs. Robinson," Krystal interrupted. "What's wrong with my mom?"

The call fell silent for a moment. "It's not your mother, Krystal. It's your sister. I guess Kathy took some kind of pills," she said at last. "Your mom went with her in the ambulance."

Mrs. Davis went to the emergency room with Krystal. Paramedics plowed by them as they entered; they jumped against the walls in the breezeway between the two sets of automatic doors to avoid a collision. When the ambulance team had scrambled by them, they strode to the reception desk, where nurses dashed and darted like aquarium fish gobbling up falling food flakes.

Krystal struggled to get the attention of several nurses before finally succeeding with one who had just dropped a metal clipboard into a slot on a rolling cabinet.

"I'm Krystal Wayne," she said. "My sister Kathy was brought in just a little while ago." The nurse smiled and nodded. "Can I see her?"

"What was the name again?" The nurse picked up a phone and punched a few numbers. She rattled off unintelligible phrases and then listened. "You'll have to have a seat. We'll call you when you can see her," she explained as she hung up the phone.

"Is she all right?" Krystal asked.

"She's receiving expert medical attention right now. Please have a seat."

Krystal and Mrs. Davis sat together and picked up waiting room magazines simultaneously. Mrs. Davis began to thumb through an old copy of *Home & Yard*, but Krystal held her magazine on her lap and gazed at the new dramatic series flickering on the elevated television set in front of her.

The television made no entry into Krystal's thought; Krystal's head turned expectantly at the approach of every person who came into the waiting room. Finally Krystal saw her mother come through the swinging doors on the other side of the nurses' station.

"They told me you were out here," she said.

"Is she all right?" Krystal asked.

Her mother gripped Krystal's hand, curled their arms together, and led her into the emergency room. A pale Kathy lay on a white-sheeted gurney in a room created by four "walls" of hanging white linen. Krystal leaned over her sister, gathered her hand in both of hers, and kissed her forehead.

Kathy opened her eyes.

"Hi, Kathy. It's Krystal."

Kathy smiled weakly and closed her eyes again.

"What happened?" Krystal asked her mother, but it was Kathy who spoke.

"I'm pregnant, Krystal," she said without opening her eyes.

THE GREAT DEBATE

'm really sorry I haven't been there for you," Krystal said
to her sister. Kathy had been transferred to a hospital room
where they were keeping her for observation and testing.

"It's not your fault, Krystal." Kathy's eyes welled with tears.
She reached for a tissue. "I was *so* depressed after breaking up
with Bill, and then . . ." She drew a swift breath and swallowed
hard. "And then when I found out that I was pregnant . . ."

"Didn't you—"

Kathy met Krystal's eyes. "Didn't I what?"

"Nothing. Never mind."

"No, you were about to ask something."

"No, I—I don't know what I was going to say."

"You were going to ask if we used protection, weren't you?"

Krystal began to speak, but couldn't find the words she wanted to say.

"Krystal, I'm not stupid."

Krystal was surprised that her sister did not sound angry, only tired.

"Look at me, Krystal." Kathy propped herself up on her elbows. Krystal returned her earnest gaze. "We *always* used protection."

* * * * *

"I don't think you understand the position you've put me in." Mrs. Caldwell, the high school principal, had called Krystal and Brad into her office at the beginning of school the Monday morning before the debate.

The posters had hung on the walls for a week, and fliers had been slipped into every windshield, desk, and locker on the grounds. The posters and fliers used a picture Joy Akiyama had drawn to symbolize the debate, showing two bighorn rams charging to butt heads with each other.

The school radio station, WEHS, had been sprinkling public service announcements about the debate throughout its broadcasting day. The debate consumed the whole front page of Friday's edition of *The General*, complete with separate interviews of Krystal Wayne and Brad Stuart. Students were talking about it in the halls. The debate had grabbed everyone's interest, and Brad and Krystal had suddenly become mini-celebrities at Ike. Mr. Detweiler had suggested, due to the enthusiasm the debate was generating, moving the event to room B1, the big lecture room, or even to the auditorium.

"Do you know how many parents have called me already this morning?" the principal asked. "I even got calls *at home* over the weekend! This has got to stop!"

Krystal and Brad had been sitting side by side, but they looked at each other now for the first time.

"This school is not a showcase for your personal social agenda," Mrs. Caldwell went on. "We're in the business of education here, not—"

"But Mrs. Caldwell," Krystal broke in. "This *is* education. That's what debate is all about, especially this debate."

"No, I don't think so, Miss Wayne. I don't think it's about education at all. I think it's about propaganda. I call it a battle about morality, not about education. And as long as this is my school—"

The phone on Mrs. Caldwell's desk emitted a high, soft sound, somewhere between a beep and a ring. She picked up the receiver.

"Principal Caldwell here." She listened. "Yes, I—" Her hard features slowly evolved into a softer expression. "I see," she said, then, "I have them right here in my office now. I'll convey the news."

She returned the phone to its cradle, but held her hand in place and tapped the receiver several times with her index finger. "That was Superintendent Edwards. He said that so many parents raised a stink about this debate that he had decided to cancel it. But I guess he talked to Mr. Detweiler, who changed his mind. Anyway, he instructed me," she continued, wearing an expression of distaste, "to tell you that he and the school board will be present at your debate this Friday."

Krystal and Brad exchanged glances again, and for the first time in several weeks, Krystal felt an affinity for Brad . . . perhaps because they were feeling the same degree of terror.

Krystal and Brad rose to leave the principal's office together; Brad stepped aside to allow Krystal to exit first. He grabbed her arm as she walked.

"Krystal, hold on."

She faced him.

"Look," he continued. "I really didn't want things to be this way."

She waited, curious. His face wore a look she didn't recognize. She couldn't identify the expression.

"Maybe we should call this off," he said.

"Call it off?" she answered, not angrily. Her tone was disbelieving. "Call it off?" she repeated. "Now?"

"We can go back into Mrs. Caldwell's office and she can call the superintendent and it will be so much easier for everyone this way."

"I can't believe this," she said, still in the same incredulous tone.

"Things have gotten out of hand," he began, but she interrupted.

"After what you've put me through these past couple of weeks—the embarrassment, the hurt—you expect me to call it off now? Why did you wait till now?"

"I never really wanted this debate, Krystal."

"Since when?" She let out a sigh of exasperation. "I can't call it off now. Do you know how much work has been put into this? Do you know what it would mean to call this off? I can't do that, Brad. I can't do it. It's too late."

As she dismissed his appeal, Krystal witnessed a change in his expression. This one she recognized; it was anger.

"Fine," he said through gritted teeth. "You want it? You got it. The debate is on."

He spun on his heels and marched away from her down the hall.

$\bullet$ $\bullet$ $\bullet$ $\bullet$ $\bullet$

The lecture room buzzed as students entered and chose their seats among the tiered desks of the amphitheater-style classroom. Narrow lecterns were positioned beside two small desks on opposite sides of the floor. Three molded plastic chairs facing the speakers bore paper signs marked "Judge."

The room was devoid of posters and banners; Mr. Detweiler had insisted on it. He told Krystal that the publicity she and her friends had generated for the debate had made him uncomfortable; he was afraid it compromised the integrity of debate.

The swelling crowd quieted slightly as Mr. Detweiler and two other teachers entered the room and folded themselves into the judges' chairs. Each of them held a folded piece of paper and a pen.

Wolf whistles, combined with light applause, greeted Brad and Krystal as they took their places at their desks; Krystal was clad in a striking but modest dress, and Brad wore his usual thin tie and creased pants.

Krystal placed both hands in her lap in an attempt to hide the trembling caused by an attack of jitters that had overtaken her several minutes ago as she waited in the next classroom. She looked out nervously at the faces in the room. Every seat was occupied; students sat in the windows behind the top row and lined the walls along the side of the room. It was a full house.

The door behind Krystal opened loudly, and Krystal turned to see Mrs. Caldwell clumsily dragging two chairs into the room. Jennifer Woolsey followed with two more and a third student carried three stacked chairs. The students who had been standing inside the door were required to move and the seven chairs were deposited there. Mrs. Caldwell ducked out the door again and returned quickly, escorting four women and three men—the school board. She offered them the new seats and stood, with her arms crossed, beside them.

Mr. Detweiler rose and faced the group. He introduced Mrs. Caldwell, the members of the school board, and the teachers serving as judges. He explained some things about debate, invited students interested in debate to meet with him

Monday after school for more information, and then—quickly, because the students were growing restless—introduced the topic and outlined how the debate would proceed. He then introduced the debaters—to a rowdy and not completely respectful ovation.

He sat down, and with a nod, signaled Krystal that it was time to begin.

"Sex with a condom used to be called 'safe sex'," Krystal began. "Have sex with anyone you want, the message went, just be sure you protect yourself. Use a condom.

"Well, things have changed now. If you pick up pamphlets at the Walnut Street Clinic *these* days, you'll find that the same clinic that used to talk about 'safe sex' *now* sings a different song: They're talking '*safer* sex.' Why the change? I'll tell you in a minute.

"Mr. Stuart and I are here today to debate a hot issue, an issue that has torn apart families, schools, and communities. My purpose will be to argue for the proposition that distributing condoms to high school students—as Mr. Stuart has advocated on various occasions—is dangerous."

She allowed herself a glance at Jason Withers, sitting in the front row to her right. He held a fist close against his chest at the level of the desk in front of him and flashed a thumbs-up signal.

She breathed deeply and went on.

"This is a condom." She held up a packaged condom in one hand. As she did, a shudder went through her, not only at the item in her hand, but at the recollection of the night she and Brad ran out of gas. She closed her eyes briefly, as the image of Brad, wielding a condom and suggesting, "Is it time for this?" assaulted her emotions. She forced her eyes open and wrestled her feelings under control.

"In some school districts," she continued, wagging the condom back and forth in the air, "they are made available to students, distributed by the school itself or by a clinic or agency. I believe that such distribution of condoms has several effects: It increases sexual activity among students, creates a false sense of safety, and fails to prevent pregnancy and disease as proponents of condom distribution contend."

She placed the condom on the desk.

"I promised a moment ago to tell you why 'safe sex' advocates have now changed their terminology to 'safer sex.' The reason for that change is that strong opposition based on medical research forced them to stop lying by calling sex with a condom 'safe sex.' Because it isn't safe. In fact, even calling it 'safer' is like calling pure street drugs 'safer.' Sex with a condom is not safer sex; it is less dangerous sex."

She thought she noticed discomfort on Brad's face, and she seized on it. "Mr. Stuart," she said, pointing at her opponent, "would like us to think that he wants condoms to be made available to high school students so that mature, independent teenagers who are ready can choose to be sexually active.

"However, a number of studies show that comprehensive sex education—which often includes distribution of condoms—if anything, may increase sexual activity among students." Krystal referred to an index card in her hand. "Dr. Robert Kistner of Harvard Medical School, who helped develop the birth control pill, said in 1977, 'About ten years ago, I declared that the pill would not lead to promiscuity. Well, I was wrong,' he admitted. If Dr. Kistner admits that the pill—one form of birth control—encouraged more sexual activity, then it shouldn't be farfetched to suppose that condoms—another form of birth control—have the same effect."

Krystal snapped the white index card to the back of the thin stack in her hands and referred to another. "Consider the results of a condom-availability program at Balboa High School in San Francisco.

"Even though condoms were distributed and students were trained in their use, the program was deemed a 'colossal failure.' Before the condom experiment began, 37 percent of the school's female students were sexually active, and the annual pregnancy rate was 5.9 percent. When the experiment ended two years later, *46 percent* of the school's female students were sexually active, and the school's overall pregnancy rate had increased to 7.4 percent per year."[1]

"Now, I ask you," Krystal said, scanning the audience and raising her voice, "if condoms are being promoted and supposedly used, why are *more* girls getting pregnant? Because they're having more sex!" She mechanically slapped the podium with these words. "Because with condoms so easy to obtain, some sexually active students are becoming more active, and those who previously had not been sexually active are encouraged to experiment."

Krystal lifted her head to look at the crowd and was startled to see every set of eyes riveted on her. She glanced at the white-faced clock on the wall.

"Um, second, the distribution of condoms among high school students would also create a false sense of safety. A teenager who is given a condom by a school official because it is a way of practicing 'safer sex' will make the assumption, 'I can *do it* safely with this.'" A few snickers hailed her emphatic use of the phrase "do it."

"After all, the student is in the habit of believing what the school says. The teacher tells him that the Battle of Waterloo took place in 1815, or that F. Scott Fitzgerald wrote *The Great Gatsby*, and he believes it. What will he do then when the same school hands him a condom and tells him it's for protection against pregnancy and disease? Will he think, *I wonder how many people get pregnant or get AIDS even though they use a condom?* No, of course not—because he's in the habit of believing what the school says.

"Finally," Krystal continued, shifting her weight to her other foot, "my third point deals with the reasons why this sense of safety provided through condoms is a false one. I'm going to tell you something you'll probably never see in a Walnut Street Clinic pamphlet. Condoms *do not prevent* pregnancy and disease." She flashed a look at her opponent.

"Does using a condom mean you won't get pregnant or wind up with a sexually transmitted disease? Absolutely not."

She fell silent, and remembering Jason's coaching, slowly scanned the audience dramatically. She flipped to the next card.

"According to pediatrician Henry J. Redd, condoms have an annual 18 percent failure rate for all teens when it comes to pregnancy. Let me put this in perspective."

Krystal surprised herself by taking a few steps away from the podium toward the crowd. "Ladies, if twenty-five of you are sexually active and using condoms as your form of birth control, four or five of you will probably be pregnant before this time next year. You may as well start picking out baby clothes!"

The audience chuckled softly, giving Krystal a chance to catch her breath.

"Dr. Redd also puts it this way," she went on. "'The annual failure rates of condoms extended through high school means that a promiscuous fourteen-year-old girl has an 87 percent chance of becoming pregnant before she graduates.'[2]

"And what about STDs—sexually transmitted diseases? Condoms are often promoted as the most effective method of preventing disease transmission during sex. That's why people refer to condoms as 'protection.' But how well do they really protect us?

"A special review panel led by the National Institutes of Health of the U.S. Department of Health and Human Services examined eight of the most common STDs—HIV, gonorrhea, chlamydia, syphilis, chancroid, trichomoniasis, genital herpes, and human papillomavirus or HPV." She paused and let out a light-hearted sigh of relief, after correctly pronouncing the words.

"The supposed *good news* is that the study revealed an 85 percent decrease in risk of HIV transmission among consistent condom users verses non-uses. I'm sure I don't need to point out that 85 percent is far from risk-free.

"The panel also concluded that condoms could reduce the risk of gonorrhea, but only for men." Krystal looked up from the index card and raised her eyebrows. "How's *that* for sexism, ladies?

"But here's the kicker," Krystal continued. "Aside from the reduction of HIV transmission, the panel's report found that, and I quote, 'epidemiological evidence is *insufficient* to determine the effectiveness of condoms in actual use for preventing *most other* sexually transmitted diseases.'[3] The report prompted Tom Coburn, a former United States Representative who is also a physician, to make the statement that 'it is medically inaccurate to say that condoms prevent STDs.'"[4]

Krystal looked at the clock, then began speaking faster. "So, with all the known consequences of premarital and extramarital sex, including but certainly not limited to disease and unwanted pregnancy, I find it hard to believe that our school board would be willing to risk the lives of the students by encouraging them to have sex using condoms.

"For these reasons," Krystal said, with another glance at the clock, "I propose that the only safe solution is found in a variation of the time-honored saying, '*Abstinence* makes the heart grow fonder.'"

She stopped and peered at the audience. A few in the room responded to her quip with quiet laughter; one of the judges even smiled. Krystal wheeled on her high heels and returned to her seat.

If it is possible for a person to leap while remaining seated, Jason did it. He squirmed in his seat with elation and flashed an approving grin at Krystal.

She sat down behind the desk like an inflatable toy that has sprung a leak. All her color and height seemed to flow out of her.

"Miss Wayne," Mr. Detweiler said, "you've overextended yourself by thirty seconds. That will be deducted from your cross-examination of the negative."

He turned his head to face Brad. "Mr. Stuart. You have one to two minutes to prepare for your first negative cross-examination of the affirmative."

A cloud of silent tension descended on the room as Brad flipped pages and jotted notes. Several people jumped nervously when Mr. Detweiler spoke again.

"One minute," he announced, and the room fell silent again.

Finally Brad stood, and with deliberate, unhurried steps approached the podium. Krystal also rose and faced Brad, grabbing the sides of the podium to still her trembling hands.

"Miss Wayne," he began. "You paint quite a picture." His accent seemed more pronounced than ever before. "You particularly challenge the educational community," he said, with a purposeful glance at the three judges. "You impugn the ability of a school that teaches history and mathematics and literature accurately and well to also be responsible in conveying complete and truthful information about condoms and their effectiveness.

Do you not see the inconsistency inherent in your remarks?" He smiled charmingly when he had finished.

Krystal suddenly felt vulnerable. Her constructive speech had been prepared carefully over the course of a week with the help of her friends. Now, alone and without notes, she was afraid and felt attacked, cornered.

"No," she said, finally. "No, Mr. Stuart, I don't." *Why don't I?* she asked herself, fighting the onset of panic. "To help you understand why," she said, speaking very slowly to buy time, "I'd like to ask you—and the judges and the students in this room—in what sex education class have you heard the information I shared in my constructive? How many of us before today have even *heard* someone talking about safe sex also talk about condom failure rates?

"But the real point of your question, Mr. Stuart, is that I think you missed my point entirely. My point is that distributing condoms to high school students does not accomplish what is intended and very often accomplishes the exact opposite—more sexually active students, more pregnant students, more infected students."

She cast a glance at the clock as she finished. *Almost through it,* she told herself. Exactly a minute remained in the three-minute cross-examination period.

"One more question, Miss Wayne. I noticed that you cited only one date in all the statistics and research you shared, and that date was 1977—before either one of us was even born. Was the rest of your information as outdated as that?"

Krystal wanted to reach for the large index cards on the

desk, but she saw the clock ticking away and knew her time was short.

"No, Mr. Stuart, it isn't. I suppose I should have cited all dates for your benefit, but as it turns out, I had too much information to fit into my six-minute time period and ended up going over. What that 1977 date may indicate to you, however, is that some of the information I shared has been around for a long time, and yet it has been apparently ignored—or even covered up—by those who support your position, for whatever reason."

The two debaters faced each other, motionless, for a few moments. Finally, Mr. Detweiler broke in.

"Mr. Stuart," he said, "do you wish to prepare for your negative constructive?"

Brad sighed and nodded. He returned to his seat and began rapidly writing, sorting index cards, and shuffling papers. Krystal also sat and began organizing her notes.

Mr. Detweiler had announced the completion of the first minute of Brad's preparation time and cleared his throat to announce the end of the second minute when Brad stood and strode to the podium.

Krystal looked up from her notes. She tried to remember her handsome, blue-eyed opponent as a friend, as something more than a friend. Something gripped her heart and held it like one would a sponge, squeezing, slowly squeezing something out of it.

Brad scanned the room carefully for a few moments.

"Your time has begun, Mr. Stuart," Mr. Detweiler said.

He nodded, then looked around the room and announced,

"A little more than fifty students in this room are sexually active. No, I haven't been having you followed," he said with a charming grin. "It's simple statistics. There appear to be around a hundred students here today, and statistics show that 54 percent of teenagers in American high schools are sexually experienced.[5] For high school seniors, the number jumps to 64.9 percent. Apart from everything I or my opponent may say here today, teenagers are having sex. That remains a fact.

"And we all know that adolescent sex carries its own set of dangers. Think of the young women who are getting pregnant while still in high school. Statistics currently show the teen pregnancy rate to be around 9 to 10 percent. That means about a million young women out there—some perhaps in this room— are being forced to make life-altering decisions. About a third of these women will make the tragic choice to have an abortion.[6] Others will choose to keep the baby or give the child up for adoption. But whatever they choose, teenage life as they knew it will be over.

"Perhaps the most heartbreaking statistic—" Brad stopped with a sudden intake of breath. His face reddened, and he appeared on the verge of tears. He struggled for control of his emotions.

Finally, he cleared his throat and, with a short sniff, resumed, speaking shakily at first but gaining control with each word. "The most heartbreaking statistic is that more than 15 million new cases of STD infections occur in the U.S. each year. And of those infected, one in four are teenagers. That means that in the seven minutes I have to present my position in this debate," he paused and wiped away a tear, "approximately fifty adolescents will acquire a sexually transmitted disease."[7]

Krystal glanced at Jason and rolled her eyes. *What an actor!* she thought. As she looked away from Jason to examine more of the faces in the crowded room, she feared that Brad's theatrics were working.

Brad lowered his eyes and paused again, but soon lifted his head and gazed engagingly at the crowd. "I say that to emphasize this point. Even though teenagers are aware of the risks, they are *not* practicing abstinence." He flashed a cunning smile. "And you know who you are." Several in the room chuckled, grateful for relief from the tension. When Brad spoke again, he was in full command of his voice and emotions.

"It is my purpose to refute Miss Wayne's contention that the distribution of condoms to high school students is dangerous. On the contrary, it is my belief that *not* distributing contraceptive means of birth and disease control is far more dangerous.

"Miss Wayne would have you believe that handing a condom to a teenager will trigger a happy-go-lucky sex spree that will continue so long as condoms are available.

"The former Surgeon General of the United States would disagree." He changed index cards swiftly. "Dr. David Satcher, in his July 2001 report on responsible sexual behavior said in no uncertain terms that 'providing information about contraception *does not increase* sexual activity, either by hastening the onset of sexual intercourse, increasing the frequency of sexual intercourse, or increasing the number of sexual partners.'[8]

"And Susan Motamed of Planned Parenthood had this to say: 'Contrary to the assertions of abstinence-only supporters, balanced and responsible sexuality education does not encourage teens to start having sexual intercourse or to increase their frequency of sexual intercourse. In fact,' she said, 'research has shown that programs that include information about delaying intercourse and about contraception can delay the age of first intercourse, reduce the frequency of intercourse and decrease the number of sexual partners teens may have.'"[9]

Brad paused for a moment, letting his words sink in. He glanced again at his note cards. "And what about Miss Wayne's contention that condoms create a false sense of safety and that they do not prevent pregnancy and STDs? Well, those are interesting opinions, but they are not grounded in fact.

"In an HIV/AIDS Prevention Training Bulletin, the Centers for Disease Control and Prevention asserts that sexually transmitted infections are preventable. 'The latex condom,' they maintain, 'provides a continuous mechanical barrier which affords excellent protection against a wide variety of bacteria, viruses, and other germs. Aside from preventing HIV infection directly, widespread condom use could have a substantial indirect impact on the HIV epidemic by preventing other STDs, some of which increase the risk of HIV transmission.'[10]

"A 1992 study on the effectiveness of latex condoms as a barrier to HIV-sized particles found that using a condom during intercourse is more than ten thousand times safer than not using a condom.[11]

"And two studies from the early 90s," Brad went on, only glancing at his notes, "determined that condoms are 98 percent effective in preventing pregnancy when used correctly[12] and up to 99.9 percent effective in reducing the risk of STD transmission when combined with spermicide.[13]

"And consider the results," Brad continued, "of a study published in The New England Journal of Medicine. For an average of twenty months, the researchers tracked 124 heterosexual couples where one partner was HIV-positive and the other was HIV-negative. Of the 124 couples that used condoms consistently and correctly, no seroconversion occurred. That means that *not one* of the uninfected partners received the HIV virus from their infected partner when condoms were used."[14]

Brad took a handkerchief out of his pocket and wiped his brow. "Or take for instance the report Miss Wayne cited from the National Institutes of Health. If you read it carefully and without bias, you'll find that the report only says that the studies are *inconclusive* as to determining the effectiveness of condoms in preventing non-HIV sexually transmitted diseases. As for HIV, the report even says that the latex condom is a 'highly effective' method for preventing transmission of the virus. But with the other seven diseases studied, Miss Wayne is interpreting a lack of evidence to mean that the research proves condoms to be *ineffective*, and that simply isn't the case.

"Here's what the panel *said*," he continued. "'The absence of definitive conclusions reflected inadequacies of the evidence available and *should not* be interpreted as proof of the adequacy or inadequacy of the condom to reduce the risk of STDs.'"[15]

Brad took his eyes from his note cards and stared intently at the audience. With a shrug of his shoulders, he continued. "It seems Miss Wayne is so short on real evidence, that she has to look for evidence that isn't there."

With this remark, Krystal's head shot up from her own note-taking. It was all she could do to keep from jumping out of her seat to give Brad a piece of her mind. She glanced at Jason in the audience, who made a reassuring gesture with his hands, as if to say, *Just keep it together, Krystal. You'll have your chance.*

With a dramatic air, Brad put his note cards away on the podium and took a few steps toward the audience. He cleared his throat and began speaking in a softer tone of voice, as if he were just sharing his thoughts with a close friend.

"Look," he began. "Nobody's saying that condoms are perfect. Miss Wayne is correct that they don't completely eliminate the risk of pregnancy or sexually transmitted disease. But they are certainly better than no protection at all.

"The Centers for Disease Control, the U.S. Department of Health and Human Services, the Sexuality Information and Education Council of the United States, have all advocated condom use as being a highly effective method for reducing the risk of pregnancy and disease. So I ask my opponent," Brad turned toward Krystal, "why would they do this if condoms weren't safe? Is this some kind of government conspiracy to trick American kids into having sex? What possible motivation could they have?"

Again, Krystal scowled at her opponent. It seemed Brad

was getting awfully personal, but she held her emotions in check.

"Maybe it would be nice," Brad continued turning back to the audience, "if everyone had the moral fortitude to abstain from sex until they were married. But anyone who has been in an American high school since Roosevelt was president must certainly agree that this is extremely unrealistic—teenagers *are* having sex. Study after study confirms that fact. And we all know the dangers that could face them *if* they are uninformed and ill-protected.

"I guess what I'm trying to say is that condoms can save lives. And I find it difficult to understand why my opponent would be willing to risk students' lives to satisfy her particular moral agenda. You see, it would be the height of irresponsibility and callous indifference to stand idly by and let our friends and sons and daughters become infected and die because we withheld protection from them.

"Few parents want their children to go to war. But if they enlist, what caring adult would suggest they do so without the items designed for their protection—helmet, rifle, flak jacket?

"Yet American parents send their children out every day into a society that, in most cases, withholds the protection they need. . . ." Brad paused and glared at the crowd in the room. "The protection they could die without."

He stood motionless for a long, agonizing moment, then turned, picked up his note cards, and walked stiffly back to his chair.

Krystal had set her pencil down quietly on the desk to

listen to Brad's summary. As he returned to his chair, she again looked to Jason for encouragement. Jason was not looking at her. He was biting his lip.

THE STATE OF THE DEBATE

K rystal suddenly felt tired. She had been taking notes during Brad's constructive—what debaters call "flowing"—and now she just wanted to lay her head down on the desk and rest.

"Miss Wayne." The voice of Mr. Detweiler jolted her from her lethargy. "Your cross-examination of the negative will be two and one-half minutes."

She nodded. *If I could just take a two-minute nap*, she thought, aware that the timekeeper had begun clocking her one- to two-minute preparation time. Without looking at the clock, however, she inhaled deeply, let out a sigh, and wearily gathered her notes. Stepping to the podium, she began.

"Mr. Stuart," she began, "you cited a Planned Parenthood study which determined that sex education programs including information about delaying intercourse can actually *delay* the age of a young person's first sexual encounter. Is that correct?"

Brad nodded. "Programs that include information about contraception *and* about delaying intercourse, yes."

Krystal pressed on. "You seem to think that teenagers are incapable of controlling themselves when it comes to sex. Doesn't this study make it clear that teenagers are not just mindless vessels of raging hormones? That, when trusted with information about the concerns and dangers of teenage sex, young people actually *can* control their behavior?"

A segment of the audience burst into a brief round of applause.

Brad seemed a little rattled, but only for a moment. "Well, it shows that sexuality education programs have an impact. And it shows that teenagers *are* making choices about their sexuality. But realistically speaking, very few are making the choice for total abstinence. And when they do decide to have sex, we need to make sure they have access to the protection that could save their lives and the life of their partner."

Brad's answer was met with another round of applause, and Krystal felt sure it was louder than the applause she had received. This time, Mr. Detweiler stepped in and asked the crowd to hold their applause.

When Krystal looked back at her note cards, she couldn't

find her place. She began searching frantically through the papers and cards.

"But," she said falteringly. She was having trouble getting her fingers to cooperate, and finally gave up. "I must admit that I agree with a very important statement you made a moment ago. You said that parents are sending their children out into society without the protection they need. Am I quoting you accurately?"

Brad's eyes searched her expression. "Yes," he answered, then added, "protection they could die without."

"I could not agree more. However," Krystal said, dropping her notes and stepping to the side of the podium, "you and I disagree on what form that protection should take."

She pointed a finger at Brad. "You think that all a teenager like you—" A tiny squeak of emotion escaped her lips. She took a quick breath and started over. "You think that all a teenager like you or I need is a thin piece of protection against disease. But what we really need is to understand, when someone tells another person that love makes it right, is that he or she is saying love makes it okay to simply have sex. The truth of the matter, Mr. Stuart, is that real love *does* make it right. Because love says, 'I'll wait for the context of a lifelong commitment of devotion and loyalty to express the beauty of sexual intimacy.' Sex without commitment isn't a love builder—it's a love killer. And that's what every student in this country needs protection from—don't you agree, Mr. Stuart?"

Krystal punctuated each word with emotion as she struggled to hold back tears. Mr. Detweiler cleared his throat sternly. "Mr. Stuart," he said, "you may have time to respond to that—" he hesitated—"that question."

The tips of Brad's ears reddened slightly. He didn't smile. "I don't believe Miss Wayne's, em, question warrants an answer." He cleared his throat. "I don't believe it addresses her proposition." The three judges wrote furiously. The room was silent except for the scratching of their pens on paper.

"Miss Wayne." Mr. Detweiler spoke with an edge to his voice. "The one- to two-minute rule is in effect for your preparation for your first rebuttal."

That was stupid, Krystal told herself. *You wasted that whole cross-examination spouting off like a jilted schoolgirl and getting way off the subject. Not to mention embarrassing yourself.* She was afraid to look at the faces of the crowd. *Well*, she consoled herself, *at least there are just a few more minutes to go. Then you can crawl into the nearest hole and never come out.*

She took a few moments at the podium to make sure her notes were in order this time. She placed a quivering hand at the base of her neck and swallowed hard.

"Let me begin, Mr. Stuart, by going back to the issue of the condom's effectiveness in preventing HIV. You cited a particular study from the New England Journal of Medicine. I believe you said that researchers followed 124 couples in which one partner was HIV-positive and one was HIV-negative. You said that these couples all used condoms consistently and correctly, and that in this particular research project not one of the HIV-positive test-subjects passed the disease on to his or her partner."

She paused and stole a glance at Brad. His hands were folded under his chin, elbows planted on the desk. He didn't look directly at her, but answered her implied question with a nod.

"Well, I'm familiar with this particular study," she continued. "Your facts are basically correct, but incomplete. And I'm afraid they are misleading."

Now Brad looked at her. "You see," she went on, "researchers didn't just observe 124 couples. They actually tracked 245 couples in which one of the partners was HIV-positive. You're correct in saying that in this particular study the 124 couples who used condoms consistently and correctly did not transfer the virus. But what happened to the other 121? As I'm sure you must know and just chose not to mention, 121 couples failed to use condoms consistently and correctly. Despite frequent counseling, and even though they *knew* one of the partners was HIV-positive and the other was at risk!

"And of the 121 couples," Krystal continued, "who did not use condoms for *every* sexual encounter or who did not use them correctly, 10 percent of the HIV-negative partners became infected.[1] I know it must sound a little like I'm suddenly endorsing condom use. Actually, what I'm trying to do is point out one more danger of relying on condoms instead of abstinence, and that is that people don't tend to use them consistently.

"I'm sure all of the HIV-negative partners in the study had good intentions of using condoms every time. Still, when it came down to actual practice, only 50 percent used condoms consistently and correctly. The rest are now paying the tragic price.

"In all the literature claiming that condoms reduce the risk of pregnancy and disease, the one caveat is that the condoms must be used consistently and correctly. Yet, according to the CDC, research shows that only 30 to 60 percent of men who claim to use condoms for contraception actually use them for every act of intercourse.[2] A study of nineteen-year-olds showed that only 39 percent reported always using a condom.[3]

"And even among consistent condom users, incorrect use is common. The Medical Institute for Sexual Health, in a study of male college students who used condoms consistently, found that one in three were exposed to pregnancy or STD risk in the prior month. The majority of these experiences were due to incorrect use.[4]

"Friends," she said, looking up from her notes, "I'm not saying that condoms break or leak or slip off every time. But once is all it takes. And whether the condom fails the person, or the person fails to use the condom, the results could be deadly.

"Now," she said with a sidelong glance at Jason, noticing that Duane Cunningham had slipped into the room and crouched on one knee beside Jason's desk. "Let's get back to the condom's effectiveness—or should I say 'lack of effectiveness'—for preventing STDs *other than* HIV."

She shuffled her index cards again. "As I mentioned earlier, the National Institutes of Health revealed that condoms could not be proven to be effective in preventing non-HIV diseases. Mr. Stuart," she said, looking at Brad, "you believe these results are purely accidental, that the evidence is merely inconclusive. But ask yourself, Mr. Stuart, 'why is the evidence inconclusive?'

"The main reason," she continued, "is probably because many STDs are transferred by skin-to-skin contact, by areas not covered by a condom. Take, for instance, HPV—human papillomavirus. It's the most common STD, infecting an estimated 20 million Americans. HPV is the cause of nearly all cervical cancer and has also been linked to other kinds of cancer. And yet, there is no evidence that condom use reduces the risk of HPV infection."[5]

Krystal moved one note card to the back of the stack to read from another. "Here's what the Medical Institute for Sexual Health says: 'We do not know exactly what effect condom use has on HPV infection risk, but in theory condoms should *not* be very effective. HPV infection is spread by skin-to-skin contact and the virus is frequently present throughout the genital region of infected people—including those areas not covered by the condom. Infection may be transmitted or contracted even when condoms are used consistently and correctly—100 percent of the time.'"[6]

Krystal glanced impatiently at the clock. "I see that my time is running out. But let me just point out that HPV is not the only STD that is transmitted by skin-to-skin contact. Other examples are syphilis and genital herpes. And condoms have little effect on these kinds of diseases.

"And lastly," Krystal went on, speaking quickly, "keep in

mind that not all STDs are equal. Some are more infectious than others. The HIV virus is not considered highly infectious. In other words, it takes a higher infectious dose or number of organisms to produce HIV infection. Other STDs, like gonorrhea and chancroid, and even the deadly HPV, can be transmitted with relatively low doses, so they are considered highly infectious.

"Again, the Medical Institute for Sexual Health points out that even when condoms are used, the risk of transmitting disease can be quite different for different kind of infections. 'Real risk of infection does exist,' they write, 'because condoms—even when used consistently—do fail. Highly infectious STDs are less "forgiving" of condom failure. Therefore, even one episode of condom breakage or slippage may expose one to a significant risk of contracting a highly infectious STD.'"[7]

Krystal bowed and left the podium just as her time ran out. She caught Duane's eye. He winked. Jason stuck his tongue out at her in an attempt to lighten her spirits.

Mr. Detweiler began Brad's preparation time for the negative rebuttal, his final opportunity to speak. Brad sat back in his chair. Occasionally he would jot a few words on his yellow pad, but most of the time he leaned back and stared thoughtfully at Krystal.

She was aware of his gaze, but did her best to ignore him. *Three more minutes,* she told herself. *Just get through Brad's rebuttal and then you only have to talk for three more minutes and it's all over. You can call Mom and ask her about transferring to a new school . . . or a new country.*

The thought of her mother reminded her of Kathy. The

picture of her sister in a hospital bed, pale and depressed, rose in her mind. *Poor Kathy. All this time I've resented her because her life seemed so "perfect." I should have been listening to her and sharing my faith with her.* She realized with a jolt that Brad had already begun his rebuttal. *How much have I missed?* she wondered.

"So you see," he was saying, "Miss Wayne and I look at this whole issue through different glasses. I prefer to look at the problem through the clear lenses of reality."

He grinned enchantingly, as though someone in the room had just complimented him on his clothes or his hair. "Miss Wayne chooses to approach the issue wearing rose-colored glasses." He leaned an elbow on the podium and slid a hand easily into his pants pocket.

"I think it's better to acknowledge the problem and *then* apply our reason and resources to its solution. Miss Wayne, and others like her, hope that ignoring the problem or wishing it away will make it disappear.

"I'm sorry, Miss Wayne. The bubonic plague didn't disappear because of good intentions. Scurvy wasn't overcome by preventing people from sailing the seas. No, in both cases, society defeated a threat by facing reality and making hard decisions, decisions that at first may have seemed preposterous."

Brad paused and changed his tone of voice. "I think it all comes down to an issue of trust. I mean, my opponent even admits that condoms do reduce the risk of pregnancy and of transferring at least *some* STDs, including HIV. But the trouble is, Miss Wayne doesn't trust students—you or me—to handle that information. She doesn't trust us to be able to use the resources we have available to protect ourselves and our partners. So she'd just prefer we hide our faces from the problem, pretend that students *aren't* having sex, and those who do will just have to take their chances.

"I agree that we—students, I mean—haven't had a great track record in using condoms consistently and correctly. And that puts us all at risk. But that's precisely why we *need* sexuality education that addresses the problem head on. We need a program that acknowledges what the real issues are and deals with them in a realistic way. In other words, a program that makes condoms available and clearly explains how to use them.

"We need programs," he continued, glancing at his note cards, "like the one started by Joseph Fernandez, former chancellor of the New York City schools. His HIV-AIDS education program has become a model for the rest of this country. He instituted, in that city racked with AIDS and other sexually transmitted diseases, a thorough educational and disease-prevention program of condom distribution in the high schools. But, Miss Wayne, it is a program that also provides instruction in responsible sexual and reproductive behavior.

"The New York City plan has enlisted the support and participation of parents, students, teachers, and board members, and it draws upon the resources of the city's health department to produce a progressive and effective curriculum."

Brad addressed Krystal but focused an intense gaze on the members of the school board. "In my view, Miss Wayne, and

I dare say in the view of many my age who might otherwise be victimized by unwanted pregnancies or ravaged by AIDS, Chancellor Fernandez is no longer merely an educator; he is a hero.

"Today," he continued, turning toward the audience, "we've heard a lot of scare tactics and moralistic propaganda from my opponent regarding sexuality education that promotes condoms. But let's talk about what we *haven't* heard. We haven't heard an alternative. We haven't heard one shred of evidence that abstinence-only sexuality education programs have been effective.

"Why? Because they are clearly impractical. I said it in my opening statement, but I think it's worth repeating: young people are having sex. We live in the twenty-first century, and cultural views and attitudes about sex have changed. So education must change with it. If it doesn't—if we insist on forcing an abstinence-only education down the throats of students who will not heed the message—then we have quite willingly and knowingly put our students at risk."

Brad dropped his note cards and moved to the side of the podium. "Miss Wayne, fellow students, distinguished school board, the sad truth is that an estimated 50 percent or more sexually active single people in the United States are actively carrying an STD right now, and many don't even know it. If we don't do something to protect students, the problem will only get exponentially worse, taking the lives of far too many and radically changing the lives of others.[8]

"We all know that condoms are not the only solution to the problems we face. We know that they are not even the best solution. But if we do not use the weapons we have—and condoms are among those weapons—then we are placing ourselves, our families, and our friends at risk.

"Right or wrong," Brad continued, his voice impassioned. "Young people are not waiting. They're having sex. And if we don't help them protect themselves, they won't just be having sex. They'll be having deadly sex. And to fail to give them the protection they need—the protection they could die with-out—would be beyond irresponsibility. It would be—immoral.'"

Brad turned his attention to the members of the school board seated by the door. "Thank you," he said. His eyes scanned the faces in the crowded room and finally settled on the three judges. "Thank you," he repeated.

Krystal looked without thinking and noticed several school board members nodding appreciatively. The judges all wore smiles.

●　●　●　●　●

"Go away!" Ratsbane screeched at Belchabub. "I'm trying to think!"

Belchabub waddled off in his clumsy armadillo way and left Ratsbane staring at the PIT console, transfixed by the events of the debate.

"That's it," he whispered at the screen. "That's it! I've been so blind not to see it before. Belchabub," Ratsbane screamed, "get over here!"

Ratsbane's mandibles, the pincer devices extending from

his ant mouth, worked back and forth in thoughtful rhythm as he stared back at the screen.

"I've found the second prong to the strategy," he said, thinking out loud to himself. "The first is to convince worthless human adolescents that love makes sex okay. But if that were our only strategy it would be inadequate. We would lose many important battles because some potential victims would still fear pregnancy and disease."

His ebony eyes sparkled now like twin black gemstones. "Belchabub!" he screeched, "where are you?"

The waddling figure had not reached his station on the cavern floor yet. He turned carefully, so as not to lose his balance, and began plodding back to the PIT platform.

"So," Ratsbane continued talking to himself, "if we can also convince these humans that *condoms make sex safe*, they'll have more sex and by having more sex we have a greater chance of killing their love." He shivered with demonic joy at that thought. "Oh, if we can win this debate, it's going to pay off big in the next few months!"

"Why?" Belchabub asked. He had arrived—upright—at Ratsbane's side.

"You really are as dumb as you look, aren't you?" Ratsbane said.

Belchabub blinked stupidly.

"This day will have an impact on all the teenagers of Eisenhower High. If we can win this debate, more humans will believe condoms make sex safe and responsible, and more of them will keep on having sex, sex, sex!"

"Why do we like that?"

Ratsbane stared disbelievingly at his assistant, eyeing Belchabub's hard shell. "If you weren't too much trouble to eat, you'd be drool on my chin right about now."

"But I still don't understand how condoms are going to kill love. If your lies about condoms encourage them to have sex, won't that just fuel the flames of love among them?"

"No!" Ratsbane screamed. "Our job is to help these hormone-filled adolescents confuse the intensity of sex with the intimacy of love. It's the Enemy's 'love-others-as-yourself' kind of love we're out to kill. Like that insufferable girl said, 'Sex without commitment isn't a love builder—it's a love killer!' So we must get them to believe using condoms makes sex safe and is, you know, 'the responsible thing to do.'" Ratsbane's eyes gleamed hellishly. "You see, if condoms are seen as safe and responsible, they'll keep having sex without a marriage commitment and they'll kill the Enemy's love they so desperately seek."

"That's cruel!" Belchabub said with a hellish grin.

"Exactly," Ratsbane answered proudly.

* * * * *

"You drew some interesting analogies in your rebuttal, Mr. Stuart," Krystal said as she occupied the podium for the last time. "Inaccurate—but interesting, nonetheless.

"You tried to compare the current teen sexuality crisis in this country with the bubonic plague and scurvy. I must point out that those diseases were conquered because people decided that it was important enough that they change their behavior. The plague was related to unsanitary conditions; it was reversed when people changed to responsible sanitary practices. Likewise, scurvy stopped being a threat to sailors when they changed their diet to include fruits and vegetables.

"Mr. Stuart, I agree that there is a crisis of teenage pregnancy and disease brought on by teen sexuality. And I submit that the answer—as it was with scurvy and the bubonic plague—is in a change of behavior. But rather than fight for the only real solution—abstinence until a completely monogamous commitment is begun—you choose to ignore reality and encourage others to adopt what can be termed, at best, 'less dangerous sex.'"

She returned her full gaze to the audience. "Just a couple more points in summary," she added. "The gist of Mr. Stuart's message here today has been that kids are going to have sex anyway, so we should protect them as best we can. I believe he has good intentions, but ultimately, it's the wrong approach.

"I agree with Dr. John Whiffen of the National Physicians Center who said, 'The only way we are going to help the sexually active kid is to tell him to stop being active, because the practical fact is they will get a disease if they continue to be sexually active.'

"You see," Krystal continued. "Condoms do not make sex safe. Even in the best case scenario, where sexually active teens use condoms for every act of intercourse and use them correctly every time—and mind you this is the exception rather than the rule—even then, condoms do fail. And they leave people at risk for teen pregnancy and deadly diseases."

Krystal looked at the clock and sighed. "But what I hope I can get across before I close is that even if condoms were 100 percent effective and safe, they are still not the right approach to teenage sexuality. You see, sex outside of marriage does not only have physical consequences. The emotional and spiritual consequences are even greater. And a condom offers *no* protection against that."

Krystal paused and was aware that everyone was hanging on her words. She set her cards aside and began to speak from the heart. "I'm not going to preach to you. But I believe in a creator who loves me—and you too. He created sex as a beautiful and powerful expression of love between two people who are committed in a lifetime relationship. And he put those boundaries around sex, not to spoil our fun, but to protect us from harm and provide us with the very best life has to offer. And when we step outside of those boundaries, we're the ones who hurt."

She felt the tears well up in her eyes, but pressed on. "I know, because I've been there. And I don't want any of you to have to go through that before you learn that God's way is the best."

Krystal discreetly wiped her tears. "Distributing condoms to students is dangerous." Her voice had the edge of emotion under control. "It increases sexual activity among students, it creates a false sense of safety, and it fails to prevent pregnancy and disease. But most of all, it is dangerous because it encourages a behavior that is not in the best interests of the students."

Krystal turned and made eye contact with one of the

school board members. "The best way to prevent teen pregnancy and disease, and all the heartache that accompany them, is to save sex for the context of a lifetime commitment in marriage. Please don't let our students settle for anything less." She shuffled her papers together and turned to resume her seat, but stopped suddenly and stepped back into the podium.

"Thank you," she said.

Everyone in the room exchanged puzzled glances. *What do we do now?* they seemed to be wondering.

Krystal hesitated a moment, then returned to her seat. She looked at the judges. None of them returned her gaze.

An uncomfortable feeling quickly overcame her, like the feeling she got after trying to read in a moving car. The room felt stuffy and airless, like a tomb.

Mr. Detweiler stood to face the crowd.

"The judges will take about five minutes to tabulate the results. They will be announced—" he looked at the clock. "At 4:20."

▶ THE INSIDE STORY ◀

The Great Condom Debate

The story of Krystal and Brad—and their debate—is fiction, of course. But the information, quotes, and statistics they have presented are authentic. They were not made up.

In fact, there is a huge debate raging in our society and our educational systems about the false messages that are constantly being sent to junior high, high school, and college students about sex and responsibility in the age of rampant sexually transmitted disease.

Several years ago, I gave a talk during "Safe Sex Week" at the University of North Dakota. The auditorium was jammed to capacity—about 3,000 students. As I often do in an opportunity such as that, I opened my talk with a statement that sent a rumble of discomfort through the crowd: "You've been brainwashed!"

When the students settled down, I continued. "You've had an entire week of 'safe sex' indoctrination," I said, "speakers, experts, videos, films, classes, and symposiums. You've been challenged, motivated, encouraged, indoctrinated, and pressured about using condoms to ensure safe sex. To top it all off, you were given a 'safer sex packet.' But you've been lied to."

At that point the crowd was becoming a little indignant with me. Then I lowered the boom with one question: "After all the information on 'safer sex' you have received this week, how many of you heard this week the statistical failure rate of the condom?" *Not one hand went up!* Suddenly the auditorium was as quiet as a cemetery. They looked at each other with expressions of astonishment. They realized they hadn't been told the whole truth about 'safer' sex.

I have received the same response from thousands and thousands of students. It happened at the University of Michigan with 2,500 students and at Auburn University with almost 8,000 students. Northwestern University in Evanston, Illinois, was in the midst of a push for on-campus condom machines just before I came to speak. There were newspaper articles, editorials, symposiums, and debates. Even Dr. Ruth had spoken there. But when I posed the question about knowing the statistical failure rate of condoms, not one student in the crowd of 1,400 raised a hand.

I want to explain to you the truth about condoms. In telling you the truth, I hope that I will also provide you with ammunition to confront "The Great Condom Debate" when it creeps up in your school or community.

CONDOMS FAIL TO PREVENT PREGNANCY

Does use of a condom guarantee safety from unwanted pregnancy? As Krystal Wayne brought out in her debate with Brad Stuart, *No!*

According to a Planned Parenthood report, out of a hundred women whose partners are using condoms, about fourteen will become pregnant in the first year of typical use. "Typical use" refers to the fact that most condom users do not use them for every sexual encounter, and sometimes use them incorrectly. In "perfect use," two out of a hundred will become pregnant. That means that even when condoms are used consistently and correctly, there are still no guarantees of protection from pregnancy.[9]

The above statistics were for women of all childbearing ages. But if you look at the data specifically for teenagers in the first year of typical condom use, you'll find the failure rates increase to 18 percent, and upwards of 30 percent among certain minorities.[10]

In other words, according to the above research, if you are a teenager expecting to prevent pregnancy with a condom, you're taking an 18 to 30 percent chance of being surprised sometime in the next twelve months—with a baby!

Why do condoms fail so often? There are several reasons, some involving defects or problems with the condoms themselves and others involving the individual's failure to use a condom properly or consistently. Condoms have a tendency to break, slip partially or completely off during intercourse, or leak from the base. Less common, but feasible, is the potential for organisms to leak through tiny holes in the latex barrier of the condom. (The FDA allows three to four holes per thousand condoms).[11]

Studies show the rates for condoms breaking or slipping completely off to be about 2 to 4 percent for most users. This rate may seem low, but consider this. After one hundred episodes of intercourse with a 3 percent breakage and slippage rate, 95 percent of individuals will have experienced at least one break or slip, rendering the condom practically useless for that encounter. And, as Krystal Wayne pointed out in her arguments, it only takes once to become pregnant or contract a deadly disease.[12]

Another reason for condoms' ineffectiveness is that they are not always used properly or completely. A strict set of guidelines must be followed for condoms to reach their maximum effectiveness, and research shows that very few condom users follow all guidelines.

A study of 360 female family planning clients illustrates this point. All the clients reported using condoms as their primary method of contraception for at least one month. Their habits of condom use were compared to five key behaviors considered significant in making condom use effective. Only 1 percent always engaged in all five behaviors. Twelve percent engaged in four criteria, 24 percent in three criteria, 28 percent in two, and 21 percent engaged in only one of the criteria.[13]

Even those who have "good intentions" of using condoms consistently fail to do so every time. Research indicates that only 30 to 60 percent of men who claim to use condoms for contraception actually use them for each act of intercourse. And among adolescents, consistent condom use is even lower, ranging from approximately 5 to 40 percent.[14] Common sense says that condoms provide little protection when used intermittently, and yet "intermittent" describes the habits of most condom users.

CONDOMS FAIL TO PREVENT DISEASE

The worst news is that condom failure rates regarding pregnancy only provide a small glimpse into their failure to prevent disease. That's partly because pregnancy can only occur a few days per month, while STDs can be transmitted at any time. In order to stop the spread of sexually transmitted disease, condoms would have to work ten times better for disease prevention than they do for birth control. But they don't.

Condoms have their highest success rate with infections (such as HIV) that are passed through bodily fluids. But according to Richard W. Smith, a former Venereal Disease Investigator, trusting condoms to prevent even HIV can be risky. "While HIV is only .1 microns in size, sensitive laboratory tests revealed naturally occurring defects in latex in a range of 5-50 microns, which is 50-500 times the size of HIV! . . . The FDA admits that their testing procedures could *not* detect defects in the range of 1-10 microns, which is 10-100 times larger than HIV."[15]

Dr. Susan Weller, in examining the results of ten studies involving the effectiveness of condoms in preventing the spread of HIV/AIDS, found an average failure rate of 31 percent. "The failure rate for the condom regarding AIDS is as high as 31 percent," she said, "with a disease that is 100 percent deadly. That is a long way from being safe!"[16]

Also, a 1995 study showed that "of 162 women who had sex with HIV positive men, thirty-one developed HIV in spite of the fact that they always used condoms."[17]

Keep in mind that HIV protection is the *strongest* case for condom promoters and users. In laboratory testing, condoms do not perform nearly as well in reducing the risk of other diseases such as genital herpes (HSV), human papillomavirus (HPV), and chlamydia. These diseases infect millions of Americans each year. HPV is the most common STD, currently plaguing an estimated 20 million Americans. It is the cause of nearly all cervical cancer—which kills nearly five thousand women each year—and necessitates tens of thousands of others to go through painful surgical procedures.

It is not completely clear why HSV, HPV, and chlamydia so effectively breech the barrier provided by condoms. In part, this is due to the fact that HSV and HPV are spread through skin-to-skin contact, in areas that are not covered by condoms. Then, the organisms can migrate to other areas where they do their damage.

It cannot be overstated: the transmission rate for these diseases is as if condoms were not used at all.

THE ONLY ANSWER TO THE SAFE SEX QUESTION

Much more research and evidence could be cited to show that condoms do not make sex "safe." If anything, the increased sexual activity and illusion of safety that condoms often encourage can make them deadly.

With all the questions about "safe sex" and "safer sex," where are the experts urging the only real answer: abstinence? You don't often read such straight talk in newspapers or news magazines. You don't hear it on television or in the classroom. Government officials and AIDS activists are largely silent. Where are the experts with the answers?

Though you may not hear it from politicians or the media, the experts *have* spoken. Former surgeon general C. Everett Koop once said, "The country has become involved in *Condom Mania.* I don't feel particularly happy about the role I've played in that. Condoms are a last resort . . . *the only way you can avoid AIDS is through abstinence.*"[18]

The Medical Institute for Sexual Health recently made this statement: "The messages provided to young people and unmarried adults about sexual activity and condoms need to stress that abstinence from sexual activity and sex while using a condom are not equally safe behaviors. Sexual abstinence . . . eliminates the risk of both pregnancy and STD making it clearly the healthiest and preferred sexual behavior for unmarried adolescents and young adults."[18]

And the Physicians Consortium in a 2001 report makes their recommendation, pointing out the overwhelming benefits of abstinence:

As a group of more than 2,000 physicians who deal daily with the ravages of STDs and teen pregnancy, we see a simple solution: abstinence until marriage with an uninfected partner and monogamy thereafter. This is the lifetime prescription for optimum sexual health. Our position on the matter of marriage is based on medical experience as well as science. Research overwhelmingly documents the fact that abstinence until marriage is the *optimum medical model* regarding sexuality. Individuals who remain sexually abstinent until marriage are better off medically, socially, educationally, economically, and psychologically than those who have sex outside of marriage.[19]

If these health care professionals are right, why isn't abstinence more aggressively pursued and preached in schools and clinics, in the halls of government and the media? Partly because many politicians and educators believe they can't expect youth to abstain; they're not capable of resisting the pressures to have sex outside of marriage. One college student responds to that pervading view by saying, "Are we to allow 'them' to tell us that we must promote the 'safe sex' philosophy because sexual acts among the unmarried [are] inevitable and will continue to occur even without birth control availability? This is a cruel and dangerous lie.

"We, the unmarried singles, are not animals who act on physical drives. We have control over our bodies and our choices. We can choose to practice abstinence outside of marriage. . . . In fact, we SHOULD choose abstinence. It is the only acceptable means of avoiding unwanted pregnancy, disease, and disillusionment."[18]

Abstinence until marriage with a partner who has also abstained is the only safe way to prevent sexually transmitted diseases and pregnancy out of wedlock. Condoms are just not safe enough to prevent these dangers. But even if condoms were 100 percent failsafe—I hope the last two chapters have shown that they are not—I would still challenge you to abstain from sex until you are married.

Remember what I said earlier: God gave commandments such as "Flee sexual immorality," because he knew some things we didn't and because he wanted to protect and provide for us, to nurture and cherish us. That's why he ordained marriage and abstinence before marriage as his standards for his people; because, as Dr. Joe McIlhaney says, "it can be a safe harbor in the midst of the storms of life, including the threat of sex-related disease. In a marriage relationship two people form a closed circle into which STDs cannot enter as long as each remains faithful."[21]

Though much more could be said, it's time to return to Eisenhower High School and learn the results of Krystal's debate with Brad. Though

Krystal certainly has truth on her side, winning a debate involves more than simple right and wrong; the judges must take into consideration such factors as the debater's command and presentation of the facts, and his or her ability to answer each point of the opponent in rebuttal.

Krystal's ordeal is about to come to an end.

WINNERS
AND LOSERS

No one moved from the room. Muted whispers filled the moments until the three judges filed back in, faces set like pallbearers. They halted at their seats and stood uncertainly, realizing that with Brad and Krystal seated, their chairs were facing the wrong direction. Mr. Detweiler whispered in each judge's ear; they remained standing, facing the room silently as he spoke.

"I'd like to begin by thanking the participants, Miss Krystal Wayne and Mr. Brad Stuart, who did an excellent job, especially considering they had no prior debate experience. Thank you, also, to the judges for their hard work. And I thank the members of the school board for their interest. Now," he said, rattling the tally sheet in his hand. "And each of you, of course," he added suddenly, as an afterthought, "for coming to our little, uh, exhibition." He raised the paper closer to his face.

"The decision of the judges," he intoned, "awards the victory in this debate to . . . Miss Krystal Wayne."

Krystal's last name was obliterated by Jason's war-chief whoop. He leaped from his seat, ran to Krystal, picked her up out of her chair and smothered her with celebration: jumping, hugging, spinning, backslapping, dancing.

* * * * *

Ratsbane pointed his ant head at the central monitor in front of him.

"Is something wrong, Foreman Ratsbane?" Belchabub asked weakly.

"Yes, you spineless twerp! This is hell, remember? Something's *always* wrong in hell!"

The scene of Jason's jubilation at the announcement of Krystal's victory flickered on the screen.

"We lost," Belchabub said flatly.

Ratsbane twitched and considered grabbing his assistant demon by both ears and flinging him repeatedly against the cavern walls. He dismissed the thought, however, and barked a command at Belchabub. "Take that end of the keyboard."

Belchabub shuffled to the PIT controls and punched a few keys and flicked a few switches.

"Listen very carefully," Ratsbane instructed, "and do exactly what I tell you. Make no mistakes, do you hear me?"

Belchabub mumbled agreement and nodded his head rapidly up and down.

Ratsbane spun his head and spat a red wad onto the floor of the platform. "It ain't over till it's over," he said.

* * * * *

Krystal pried herself away from Jason and was immediately met by Duane, then Buster Todd, Darcelle, Joy, Amber, and Will—all awarding hugs and gushing congratulations.

"You were terrific," Will said.

"I was afraid I blew it," she answered.

Darcelle smiled proudly. "I already have some great ideas for follow-up articles in the paper. This is great!"

Rather than bask in her victory and the accolades of her friends, Krystal was distracted now by Brad, who stood with Chase Everett, listening to Mr. Detweiler in the middle of the room.

She watched as Chase stormed off, obviously angry. She interrupted something Will was saying about the information Buster had gotten from the clinic and broke away from the group.

Brad and Mr. Detweiler both looked surprised as she approached them. Mr. Detweiler stopped speaking in midsentence.

"Hi, Brad," she said, mentally kicking herself as she said it. *You've been in the same room with the guy for over an hour and you say 'Hi, Brad?'*

After a few moments of awkward silence, Brad said, "Chase and I were checking with Mr. Detweiler to see how they scored the debate and where I made my mistakes." An embarrassed look flashed across his face. "Chase had to go somewhere."

"I *know* where I made my mistake," Krystal said. "At least the biggest one."

Mr. Detweiler turned the tally sheet her direction. "Would you like to see this?"

"No," she said. "I mean I'd like to, but later, if that's okay." Mr. Detweiler nodded. She faced Brad timidly. "I was wondering if we could talk."

He wore a melancholy look. "Yeah. I was going to suggest the same thing." He looked around the room, which was still stuffed with chattering people. "Maybe we can go somewhere."

They faced each other for a few long, uncomfortable moments, neither offering a suggestion or solution. Krystal broke the silence.

"How about your car?" she said.

"My car?" Brad's voice registered shock.

Krystal blushed slightly and cast a look over her shoulder at her crowd of friends. "And maybe, if you don't mind," she said tentatively, "you could drop me home?"

Brad blinked dumbly. He faltered, then recovered himself. "Em, yeah, that would be fine."

"I'll be right back," she said. She bounced over to the

Liberation Commando crowd, still chattering among themselves. She gripped Darcelle's elbow and explained that she wouldn't be riding home with her.

She was conscious of Darcelle's eyes following her as she joined Brad at the door of the lecture room, and she knew Darcelle would be concerned; but she knew, too, that she didn't care. This was something she had to do.

The two debaters sat in the bucket seats of Brad's car, the sounds of the closing car doors echoing away into agonizing silence and mutual discomfort.

"I'm sorry," Krystal said finally. She twisted in her seat to face him better. "I . . . I probably got a little too carried away with all of this."

"Oh, em, well, it was perfectly understandable." He smiled with closed lips. He turned his head toward her. "Congratulations, by the way," Krystal looked at him as though she had forgotten she won. "You deserved to win."

"I thought I blew it. I thought they were going to give it to you."

"You did nice work answering my points. If I didn't know better, I'd say you obtained a copy of my notes somehow."

She smiled. "No, but we did figure out that you got some of your information from the Walnut Street Clinic." Brad looked away from her and stared straight ahead, through the windshield, gripping the steering wheel tightly. "We went there ourselves and just made sure we had information to counter your arguments—as much as possible, anyway."

"Krystal," he said. She shifted her head slightly to indicate that she was listening. The car fell silent again as Brad continued to stare straight ahead. A chill shook Krystal's spine and she rubbed her hands together in her lap as she waited for him to speak again.

"I—" he began, but snapped his mouth shut quickly.

Krystal noticed a rim of redness around his eyes.

He opened his mouth again. "The information I got at the clinic was, em, an afterthought. That wasn't why I went there."

She still craned forward in the tiny car, her hands clutched in her lap, watching his eyes, but unable to see into them.

"You probably don't remember," he said. "The morning we had that big argument? At school? I told you I would get tested."

Krystal noticed his arms. They were shaking.

"I did." He looked at her then. "I'm HIV positive, Krystal," he said. "I have the AIDS virus."

After a long moment of shocked silence, Krystal bridged the space between the bucket seats and sobbed in Brad's arms. It seemed to Krystal that he held her tighter than ever before, pressing her to him with such strength that her joints began to hurt, and she wished she could find a more comfortable position—but she not only refused to break his hold, she returned it.

He finally released his grasp and slumped back into his seat. The sophisticated Englishman was gone now, and Krystal remarked to herself how much Brad resembled a hurt little boy.

"I'm sorry," he said. "I didn't want to put you through all

this." He reached across her lap and rummaged in the glove compartment, finally pulling out a handful of tissues. "I haven't told anyone yet," he said before he blew his nose.

"You haven't told your parents?"

"No," he said. "You're the first."

Krystal reached for the door and cracked her window. "We're fogging the windows," she said.

The conversation halted for a few moments until Krystal asked, "What are you going to do?"

He shrugged. "What *does* one do? I suppose I'll try to make the best of it."

A thought suddenly struck Krystal and she folded her hands in her lap again. "Why did you go through with it?" she asked faintly.

"Hmm?"

"Why did you go through with the debate," she repeated, "knowing that you were infected?"

"You didn't leave me much choice, did you? I tried to get you to call it off, but you were so—well, you know." He paused. They sat in silence again. "And if I had just backed out on my own," he continued, "everyone would have wondered why. It would have made me look quite bad. And I wasn't prepared to make any public statement just yet."

Krystal sat in silence for a few moments. When she spoke, her voice was quiet and she looked through the windshield instead of at Brad. "I'm sorry, Brad. I wish you had told me all of this *then*. I wouldn't have been so stubborn about going through with it."

He smiled. The sophisticate was back. "Oh, yes. I know. But that little conversation in the hall got away from me. I was so angry. I wanted to tell you . . ."

Her eyes welled with tears. She laid her head softly on his shoulder, and they sat without speaking until Brad started the engine and took her home.

"Brad, I *want* to do this."

"You don't have to, you know. I don't want to pressure you into something you don't want to do."

They sat in Brad's car again.

"No, it's not like that," Krystal insisted. "It's not just because you're HIV positive, either. I just feel like you need me, and I want to be there for you."

They each opened their car doors at the same time and shut them, producing a single sound. He placed a hand on her back as he opened the front door of his house. He stepped back then to let her go in first.

Brad's parents leased a roomy, beautifully furnished townhouse on the north end of Westcastle. Krystal waited nervously in the vestibule for Brad to lead the way.

"Mum? Dad?" he yelled into the high ceilings.

Krystal heard nothing.

"This way," Brad said, leading her into the kitchen, through a door, and down a staircase into a large family room.

Brad's mother stitched a hooped pattern in her lap; his father peeked around a newspaper, watching a television show.

"Mum, Dad," he started. "This is Krystal Wayne, a friend of

mine—" He stopped. "A good friend of mine from school."
They smiled, and Brad's father dropped the paper and began to
stand. "No, sit down, Dad. Krystal came with me because I have
something I have to tell you." His voice broke, but he cleared his
throat and kept speaking. "And she—she knew it would be hard
for me and didn't want me to have to do it alone."

Brad and Krystal exchanged smiling glances through tears.

●　●　●　●　●

"What do you want, you mucous-munching mongrel?"
Ratsbane busily punched commands into the Prime-Evil
Impulse Transducer keyboard. The central screen of the
console showed a thirteen-year-old girl chatting with a
leather-jacketed boy in the school hallway.

The walrus-headed gorilla form of the demon Nefarius
extended a limp piece of paper to the foreman of Subsector
1122.

"Yuck!" Ratsbane exclaimed. "You got walrus slobber all
over this." He bent his head to read the message. "What!" he
screamed. "I won't stand for this. I won't, I won't, I won't, I
won't!" He jumped and stomped around the PIT platform like
a boy on a pogo stick.

"Did you read this, you sorry, stinking, slobbering syco-
phant?" Nefarius didn't answer. He stood, ape-like, within
arm's reach of Ratsbane. "You know what they're going to do?
They're putting me on drudge duty! *Me!*

"They can't be serious! If they think I'm going to spend an

eternity in hell shoveling those sulfur globs into the lake of fire, well, they better think again!

"Who are they going to find to run this subsector? I'd like to know! I may have lost that stupid debate, but who do they think can do a better job than me?"

"It's in the last paragraph," Nefarius answered.

Ratsbane's lone antenna twitched. He bowed his head to read the rest of the memo in the glow of the monitors behind him. Suddenly his head snapped up and he glared at Nefarius.

"You?!" he squealed. "You? They can't be serious! I should have mutilated you when I had the chance, you—" Ratsbane reared a fist and swung at his former assistant from Subsector 477.

Nefarius seized Ratsbane's arm at the wrist. Ratsbane's bulbous eyes widened as Nefarius twisted and squeezed, forcing him to his knobby frog knees, his face contorted with pain.

"Belchabub! Bring this drudge his bucket," Nefarius barked.

The armadillo demon lurched onto the PIT platform and shoved a bucket in Ratsbane's direction, producing a ringing noise with a clout on his head.

Wordlessly, Ratsbane skulked off, casting hateful looks back at Nefarius, Belchabub, and the giant PIT console. He entered the slime-coated, smoldering passages that twisted throughout the underworld. At a particularly dark junction, he thudded into another drudge.

"Out of my way, human-lover," he snarled.

The throaty curse that answered him captured his attention. It was familiar. He kept pace with the drudge until they entered a lighted section of the passage.

"Stygios!" he blurted as he recognized the drudge. "What are you doing down here?"

In answer, Stygios lifted the bucket he carried, identical to the one in Ratsbane's hands, and flashed a sullen expression at his former foreman.

"Hell is really hell, you know what I mean?" Ratsbane said. "It's really not fair. Who can I talk to about this? I want to know. Who can I talk to?"

"Shut up," Stygios said.

▶ THE INSIDE STORY ◀

What I Did for Love

Brad and Krystal—with all their differences and difficulties—share a common hunger: a hunger for love.

You and I are no different. We were born with a God-given need to love and be loved. It is a legitimate need in each of us that cries out to be met.

As a newborn baby, you not only wanted to be fed with milk, you wanted to be held and cuddled—you wanted to be loved. It's as if you and I have "love tanks" that need to be filled. And if your capacity for love is not met, you're experiencing hunger pangs. The more empty you are, the more hungry you become for love.

But your love appetite is for a particular kind of love. As a small child, you reached out to receive hugs and kisses and pats on the head. And that was okay for a while. But as you grew, you began to hunger deep inside for a love that accepted you for just being you. It was a hunger for a love that would wrap its arms around you and say, "No matter what you do I will always love you for just being you!" And you wanted that love to last and last and be so secure that no matter what happened, you could count on that love to always be there.

Maybe you've had that kind of love. If you have, count yourself fortunate, because most of us never knew that kind of love. As a boy growing up, I never once remember my dad ever telling me he loved me. I never felt the secure arm of a dad's hug or even the joy of hearing a father say, "You did well, son." You see, my dad was an alcoholic; I can never remember a childhood day when my dad was sober. I can never remember a childhood day when I felt loved by him.

So I know what it's like to be love-starved so much that it creates this paralyzing fear that you won't ever be loved or be able to love. And I've found the more love starved you are, the more fear you have.

That fear often comes from all the conditions that are placed on love: *I'll be loved IF I get good grades; I'll be loved IF I'm popular; I'll be loved IF I make the cheerleading squad.*

Or maybe you believe that being loved depends on how you look or what you have, like a new car or great clothes.

The problem is, your mind is not thinking all this; it happens in your emotions, in your gut. Your natural hunger for love, now filled with fear, will start driving you to greater and greater lengths to get love.

As a teenager, my emotions told me, *You can't get love at home; try gaining love and acceptance through sports.* I felt that if I could prove myself as a jock, somebody would surely love and accept me. But it didn't happen. So in my gut I felt, *If I can't get love that way, maybe I'll get an* education—*I'll prove I'm worthy of somebody's love by getting 'smarts.'* That didn't work either. I tried prestige, politics, and parties. My hunger for love and the fear that I would never be loved drove me harder and harder to get it.

Many students do exactly what I did. They try to succeed in a sport or get perfect grades or join a gang or take drugs—all in a quest for love and acceptance. For many, the gnawing hunger to know a love that says, "I love you just for being you," has led them to the "S word": *sex.*

Sex seems to be the perfect way to express love to someone. There is something about a tender kiss, a warm embrace, and all the passion that comes with sex—it seems to say, "I love you." You see it in the movies, you hear it in songs, you read it in magazines and watch it on television. Love and sex, sex and love—they go together, right? Wrong!

Sex will never fill your love tank. Never. Because sex was never designed to create love—it was made to express love. Sex was made to reinforce and communicate the kind of love that says, "I love you so much for who you are that I will nourish that love and protect that love within the context of a permanent commitment."

Sex, the way God designed it, is to be the result of a committed love relationship, not the cause of it. So for sex to be positive and do what it's supposed to do, love must be nourished and grow to maturity and *then* sex can be dynamite!

But let me tell you something. If your love tank is running on empty and you have sex with your boyfriend or girlfriend, sex is going to reinforce and deepen your emptiness. It's going to reinforce what's in your love tank. And if you have the kind of love in your love tank that "makes it right," love will cause you to wait until a permanent commitment is made within the context of marriage.

So many I've talked with haven't waited because they have bought into the demonic lie that sex would somehow give them the love they needed. One girl wrote me this letter:

Dear Mr. McDowell,

I could not break free from the bondage of having sex with Curt. It ruled my life. How cheap and dirty I had become in my own eyes.

Sex gave me the loneliest thrills I had ever experienced. It handed me fear as a gift and shame to wear as a garment. It blinded my eyes to false love and gave me a jagged tear in my heart that even now, seven years later, is still healing.

Signed: Still Healing Single

Sex was never meant to lead to the "loneliest thrills" you ever experience. It was never meant to leave you with an empty heart the morning after. Sex was never meant to be the "love killer" in your life.

Another young lady told me, "I know having sex isn't really giving me the love I need, but at least for a brief moment I feel love." What a cheap substitute. Why settle for sex when you can know the feeling of being really loved? Maybe you've experienced the love killer. Maybe you know what it's like to feel your love tanks going empty. How can you again feel real love—a love that loves you for just being you?

There is a love, some call it a perfect love—an unconditional love—that says no matter where you've been, what you look like, what you've done (or haven't done)—*I LOVE YOU*. This love is the safest love in the world. It's a love that casts out fear, that will end that awful fear that no one will ever love you for just being you. And it comes from the very Person who created love.

You can receive that perfect love that casts out fear by trusting Jesus Christ as your Savior and Lord.

Will trusting Christ remove all your fears and give you a love so complete that you'll live happily ever after? I didn't say that. You may have deep wounds and hurts from sexual abuse, physical abuse, or emotional abuse. You need time and help in order to heal those wounds. But when you trust Christ, you will find the most trusting and safest relationship possible. It may be the first time in your life that you feel safe and really loved.

Right now speak simply and sincerely to God in prayer by saying something like this:

> Lord Jesus, I want to know you personally. Thank you for dying on the cross for my sins. I open the door of my life and trust you as my Savior and Lord. Thank you for forgiving my sins and giving me eternal life. Thank you for loving me without conditions and accepting me for being me. Take control of my life, and make me the kind of person you want me to be. I love you too. Amen.

If you've prayed those words and have placed your trust in Christ, you are now a new person; in the weeks and months to come, you will change in many ways. But one thing will never change: God loves you and accepts you for being you. Tell another Christian friend of the decision you made today. If you have been a Christian and you reaffirmed your trust in Christ, share that at your youth group. You need the support and love of other believers.

AN ICE PARTY

This is crazy," Krystal told Darcelle as they drove together to Drake Park.

"Aren't all Jason's ideas crazy?" Darcelle shot back as she made the turn off Route 27 and into the park.

"I just don't see how this is going to work, Darcelle. I don't mean to be negative, but how can we have a sledding party when there's not a single snowflake on the ground?"

Jason had suggested a sledding party back in September when the Liberation Commandos brainstormed new ideas for parties. Ever since the See You at the Party pizza bash in March, the group had planned and hosted several similar events. Each party provided an opportunity for them to invite non-Christian friends to an evening that always included a simple explanation of "How to Know God Personally." The parties were never as big as the one in March, but so far at least one of their friends had come to faith in Christ at every party.

Darcelle parked behind Will's car in the circle atop Center Hill. She and Krystal joined the dozen or so others who had arrived before them, which included two kids they knew from school. Doug Cline had come at Buster Todd's invitation, and Brenda Shafer, a sophomore Joy Akiyama had befriended, also joined them.

"This is a great hill to sled on," Will said with a smile.

"Yeah," Krystal said, "if there's snow on the ground."

The group stood at the crest of a steep hill, admiring the view and wondering what they were doing there.

Finally Duane Cunningham pulled up in his pickup truck. He and Jason bounded out of the cab and called everybody over.

Duane handed grocery bags to Joy and Brenda Shafer, and instructed them to take them to the fire ring by the shelter. "That's for later," he said.

"The rest of you need to help us with these," he said as he pulled back the tarp in the truck's bed to reveal five fifty-pound blocks of ice.

"What are those?" Amber asked.

"What do they look like?" Jason asked in response.

"Ice," she answered.

"Wrong," Jason said emphatically, lifting one of the heavy blocks and setting it down on the grass. "These are sleds."

A hoot of laughter escaped Buster's throat, and several in the group began chattering questions at Jason. "Just bring them over here," he announced, leading the way to the top of the hill. "I'll demonstrate."

A moment later, Jason careened bumpily down the hill, riding a shimmering clear block of ice.

"It's a little rough right now," he reported when he returned to the top of the hill, pushing the ice block ahead of him. "It'll get better after we've gone down a few times. The grass will be smooth and wet."

For the next hour and a half, the Liberation Commandos and their guests screamed and laughed up and down the hill. The earliest arrivals were joined by Hillary Putnam, Kim Holmes, Marci Small, and Reggie Spencer, who helped Duane start a fire.

Later, while the group sat shivering and chattering on logs around the roaring fire beside the shelter, they roasted marshmallows and drank hot chocolate. Suddenly Darcelle elbowed Krystal, causing her to spill hot chocolate on herself.

"Dar," Krystal complained in an irritated tone.

Darcelle, not immediately realizing what she had done, nudged her again and pointed toward the cars.

Krystal turned and saw Brad Stuart striding toward them, his hands stuffed deep in his pockets. She jumped up and clumsily handed her cup to Darcelle, sloshing a small spot of chocolate on Darcelle's shoe. "It's Brad," she said excitedly. "I didn't tell you I invited him. I didn't think he'd really come."

Krystal trotted to Brad's side and guided him to the tight circle around the fire. "Everybody, this is Brad Stuart. I asked him to come." Reggie and Marci, who were closest to Brad and Krystal, stood and offered their seats to him and Krystal, but another voice interrupted the offer.

"Brad," Jason called. "I'd like you to sit by me." Jason's usually silly expression was gone; he was smiling slightly, not in a joking way. Brad accepted Jason's invitation; Krystal quietly squeezed next to Brad on the log.

As they sat around the fire, the conversation soon turned to spiritual things. The group listened intently as Duane told about Tony Ortiz, who had graduated from Eisenhower High last year and was attending State University on a football scholarship. Tony had been sharing his faith at a Christian athletes prayer breakfast, Duane said. Then, with no fanfare or introduction, Reggie Spencer stood.

"I want to say a few things about tonight." The former football player grabbed a block of ice from outside the circle and dropped it in front of him, next to the fire. "Some of you know what I was like a couple years ago. I'm not going to go into a lot of detail, but my family life was so bad and I was so full of resentment and bitterness that inside—" he poked his chest so hard with his finger that everyone around the circle heard the repeated thump it made—"inside I felt like this block of ice."

Reggie went on to share more of how he had felt and how,

a little over a year ago, in a McDonald's on Poplar Avenue, Duane Cunningham had helped him come to faith in Christ.

"Duane started telling me how Jesus loved me enough to die for me, and he told me that I could have a relationship with him—a relationship based on love, not fear. He made it all seem so simple. And it was.

"I don't know if I can make it as simple as Duane did. But I'll just tell you what happened to me."

Brad Stuart listened intently to Reggie's brief testimony. Krystal watched him almost the whole time Reggie spoke, and she and Brad exchanged an occasional glance. When Reggie finished, Krystal shifted on the log to face Brad fully.

"What do you think?" she asked. "Is there anything Reggie didn't make clear?"

"No," Brad said guardedly. "No, I think I understand."

"Because if you have any questions, I'd really like to answer them. I think—"

"Krystal," Brad interrupted. He smiled. "Not right now. There are some things I need to take care of before I make a decision like that."

"But Brad, you don't have to get your act together before God will accept you. He accepts you right now, just the way you are."

"That's not what I mean," he said. "There are some things I'd like to talk over before I do . . . anything." As Brad finished, he noticed that Brenda Shafer was praying with Joy Akiyama on the other side of the circle.

"What kind of things?" Krystal asked.

"About you and me, for instance. I know you've told me that your reservations about dating me aren't so much about my being HIV positive, but more now because I don't share your commitment to God. Am I saying it right?"

She nodded.

"I think we need to discuss some things so that you'll know if I, em, do what Reggie was talking about—and I'm not promising that I will—that I'm not doing it just to please you. Do you understand?"

Krystal flashed an understanding smile. She stood, stepped close to Jason (who pretended he hadn't been listening), and whispered something in his ear. Jason stole a glance at Brad, who met his glance with a half-smile.

Krystal extended her hand toward Brad. "Let's take a walk," she said.

CHAPTER 06: STALLED BY THE SIDE OF THE ROAD

1. Although *Why True Love Waits* has two coauthors, for ease of reading we will use the singular pronoun *I* throughout "The Inside Story" sections of the book. Specific anecdotes are from Josh's personal experiences.

CHAPTER 10: THE GREAT DEBATE

1. Hartigan, John D. "The Disastrous Results of Condom Distribution Programs." *Family Research Council*, March 29, 2001.

2. Redd, Dr. Henry J. "'Safe Sex' Sex-Ed a Delusion: Abstinence, moral curricula cut sexual activity, pregnancy, STDs." *The Ledger*, September 4, 1992.

3. "Scientific Review Panel Confirms Condoms Are Effective Against HIV/ AIDS, but Epidemiological Studies Are Insufficient for Other STDs." *HHS News*, U.S. Department of Health and Human Services, July 20, 2001.

4. "Safe Sex Myth Exposed by Scientific Report: Condoms Do Not Prevent Most STDs." Abstinence Clearing House, *News and Events*, July 19, 2001.

5. Motamed, Susan. "Condom Availability and Responsible Sexuality Education." www.plannedparenthood.org, 2000.

6. "Teen Pregnancy." National Center for Chronic Disease Prevention and Health Promotion, CDC.

7. Cates, W. et. al. "Estimate of the Incidence and Prevalence of Sexually Transmitted Diseases in the United States." *Sexually Transmitted Diseases* 26 (supplemental), 1996, S2-S7.

8. "The Surgeon General's Call to Action to Promote Sexual Health and Responsible Sexual Behavior," Quoted in "Sex Talk: The Surgeon General's Farcical 'Call to Action' " by Andrew Ferguson. *The Weekly Standard*, August 6, 2001, Vol 6, number 44.

9. Motamed, Susan. "Condom Availability and Responsible Sexuality Education." www.plannedparenthood.org, 2000.

10. "The Role of Condoms in Preventing HIV Infection and Other Sexually Transmitted Diseases." Centers for Disease Control and Prevention, *HIV/AIDS Prevention Training Bulletin*, February, 1993.

11. Carey, R. F. et. al. "Effectiveness of Latex Condoms as a Barrier to Human Immunodeficiency Virus-sized Particles Under the Conditions of Simulated Use." *Sexually Transmitted Diseases* 19, no. 4 (July/Aug 1992), p. 230.

12. Trussel, J. et. al. "Contraceptive Failure in the United States: An Update." *Studies in Family Planning* 21, no. 1 (Jan/Feb 1990), p. 52.

13. Kestelman, P. and J. Trussell, "Efficacy of the Simultaneous Use of Condoms and Spermicides," *Family Planning Perspectives* 23, no. 5 (Sept/Oct 1991), p. 227.

14. De Vincenzi, I. "A Longitudinal Study of Human Immunodeficiency Virus Transmission by Heterosexual Partners," *The New England Journal of Medicine*, vol. 331, no. 6 (August 11, 1994), p. 341-6.

15. "Scientific Review Panel Confirms Condoms Are Effective Against HIV/AIDS, but Epidemiological Studies Are Insufficient for Other STDs." *HHS News*, U.S. Department of Health and Human Services, July 20, 2001.

CHAPTER 11: THE STATE OF THE DEBATE

1. De Vincenzi, I. "A Longitudinal Study of Human Immunodeficiency Virus Transmission by Heterosexual Partners." *The New England Journal of Medicine* vol. 331, no. 6 (Aug. 11, 1994), p. 343.

2. "Basic Facts About Condoms and Their Use in Preventing HIV Infection and Other STDs." Centers for Disease Control and Prevention, July 30, 1993. Found on www.thebody.com.

3. Sonenstein, F. L., L. Ku, L. Lindberg, C. F. Turner, J. H. Pleck. "Change in sexual behavior and condom use among teenaged males: 1988 to 1995." *American Journal of Public Health (AJPH)*. 1998; 88: 956-959.

4. Warner, L., J. Clay-Warner, J. Boles, J. Williamson. "Assessing condom use practices: Implications for evaluating method and user effectiveness. *Sexually Transmitted Diseases* 25, 1998, pp. 273-277.

5. "Safe Sex Myth Exposed by Scientific Report: Condoms Do Not Prevent Most STDs." Abstinence Clearing House, *News and Events*, July 19, 2001.

6. "Condom Quiz: Frequently Asked Questions About Condoms." The Medical Institute for Sexual Health. *Sexual Health Update*, Vol. 8, No. 3, Fall 2000.

7. Ibid.

8. Whiffen, John. Quoted in "Hooking Up: Casual Sex Gets a New Name" by Nancy Stellabotta. *Christian Broadcasting Network, Inc.* Christianity.com 2001.

9. "Condoms." Text adapted from "The Condom." *Planned Parenthood Federation of America*, 1999. www.plannedparenthood.org/bc/condom.htm.

10. Diggs, Jr., John R., MD. January 26, 2001.

11. Fitch, J. Thomas, MD, "How Effective are Condoms in Preventing Pregnancy and STDs in Adolescents?" September, 1996.

12. Warner, D. L. and R. A. Hatcher. "Male Condoms." In *Contraceptive Technology*. 17 edition. Hatcher, R. A., J. Trussell, et. al., eds. New York, NY: Ardent Media, Inc; 1998: 325-355.

13. Oakley, et al. "Quality of Condom Use as Reported by Female Clients of a Family Planning Clinic." *AJPH*. 1993, Vol. 85, No. 11.

14. Fitch, J. Thomas, MD. "How Effective are Condoms in Preventing Pregnancy and STDs in Adolescents?" September, 1996.

15. Smith, Richard W. "Is the Condom Really Safe Sex?: A Testimonial Statement."

16. Weller, Susan. "A Meta-Analysis of Condom Effectiveness in Reducing Sexually Transmitted HIV." *Social Science and Medicine*, 36:12, 1993. Quoted in Morris, *Abstinence*, p. 110.

17. McIlhaney, Jr., Joe S., MD. SEX: *What You Don't Know Can Kill You*. Baker Books, Grand Rapids, MI 49516, pp. 85-87.

18. "Condom Quiz: Frequently Asked Questions About Condoms." The Medical Institute for Sexual Health. *Sexual Health Update*, Vol. 8, No. 3, Fall 2000.

19. Diggs, Jr., John R., MD; Hall Wallis, MD; Joanna K. Mohn, MD; Kent Jones, MD, Ph.D. "A Perspective on the Medical Implications of the Virginity Pledge Among Teens." *The Physicians Consortium*, January 5, 2001.

JOSH MCDOWELL is an internationally known speaker, author, and traveling representative for Campus Crusade for Christ. A graduate of Wheaton College and Talbot Theological Seminary, he has written more than thirty-five books and appeared in numerous films, videos, and television series. He and his wife, Dottie, live in Julian, California, with their four children.

• • • • •

BOB HOSTETLER is a writer, editor, and frequent speaker at writers' conferences and churches. With Josh McDowell he co-authored *Don't Check Your Brains at the Door* and has published hundreds of articles, sermons, stories, and cartoons. Bob edited the national youth publications for the Salvation Army for four years and has served as a pastor in churches in Ohio and now works as a freelance writer. He and his wife, Robin, have ministered together as houseparents to troubled teenagers and now live in southwestern Ohio with their daughter, Aubrey, and son, Aaron.

GET THE FACTS!

The research, documentation, and statistics used in this book are available to you and your youth group through the Josh McDowell Research Almanac and Statistical Digest. This is a resource notebook of over four hundred pages. Use it to put on a debate, to write a term paper, or just to be kept fully informed. To obtain a free brochure on this valuable resource write:

THE JULIAN PRESS
BOX 584
JULIAN, CA 92036

GOING TO COLLEGE? DON'T GO IT ALONE

Some new Christian friends are ready to meet you!

To connect with Christians and campus ministers at your college, contact Student LINC toll-free at 1-800-678-LINC (5462).

Student LINC provides a centralized database where Campus Crusade for Christ, InterVarsity Christian Fellowship, and the Navigators have pooled their information about the locations of their ministries on campuses across the United States.

Student LINC can give you the name and phone number of the leader for each group on campus.

Also, if no strong Christian group is active on your campus, Student LINC can help you start one. For more information, just give them a call at 1-800-678-LINC (5462).

DON'T LEAVE HOME BEFORE CALLING!

If you have grown personally as a result of this material, we should stay in touch. You will want to continue in your Christian growth, and to help your faith become even stronger, our team is constantly developing new materials.

We publish a monthly newsletter called **5 Minutes with Josh** which will (1) tell you about those new materials as they become available, (2) answer your tough questions, (3) give creative tips on being an effective parent, (4) let you know our ministry needs, and (5) keep you up to date on Josh McDowell's speaking schedule (so you can pray).

If you would like to receive this publication, send your name and address to Josh McDowell—**5 Minutes with Josh**, Campus Crusade for Christ, 100 Sunport Lane, Fla. 32809.